T0208422

Attitudes and Alternatives

A Collection of Contemporary One Act Plays

Paul Trupia

iUniverse, Inc.
New York   Bloomington

This is a work of fiction. All of the characters, names, incidents,
organizations, and dialogue in this novel are either the products
of the author's imagination or are used fictitiously.

iUniverse books may be ordered through booksellers or by contacting:

iUniverse
1663 Liberty Drive
Bloomington, IN 47403
www.iuniverse.com
1-800-Authors (1-800-288-4677)

ISBN: 978-1-4401-6037-0 (sc)
ISBN: 978-1-4401-6036-3 (ebook)

Printed in the United States of America

iUniverse rev. date: 08/13/2009

Attitudes and Alternatives

One-Act Plays by Paul Trupia

Attitudes and Alternatives is a collection contemporary one-act plays written by Paul Trupia. Since 2005, these pieces have been performed Off-Off Broadway and/or at the New York theatre festivals. The common theme that binds the collection is a reflection of the real-life situations, thoughts, alternatives, and the choices we make. The collection is at times humorous, at times serious, and at times a fantasy. *Attitudes and Alternatives* debates our inner thoughts with reality and considers what is going through our minds as we go through the day. Its theme is what a woman may consider as she gets ready for a date, what a man may be thinking as he gets off work for the weekend, and the wondering thoughts of participants at an office meeting or a middle aged couple walking in the park at the start of summer. In many respects, it is what we think about in the solitude of our daily commute and toss around in our minds as we try to sleep. The one exception to the theme, "Diplomacy," is simply a suggestion of a possibility.

To the actor, director, or producer the collection offers an array of characters, situations, genre, and range that allow the development and showcase of talent. The real-life situations are familiar to many and allow the performers to identify with and interpret the role as they see it. The scripts, combined with acting talent, effective direction, and technical support, have resulted in productions that are creative, entertaining, and thought-provoking.

Summary of Plays

The collection includes the following eleven plays:

"The Fourth Voice" was performed at the 2006 Samuel French Festival and at the Parker and Producers Club Theatres. A single woman in her late 20s is getting dressed up for a date. In her preparation, she confronts inner voices that any woman may hear from time to time and that, from time to time, may conflict with her own way of life. Or do they?

"Changing Times" was performed at the 2007 Samuel French Festival and in 2006 with Love Creek Productions. A middle-aged couple react to the signs of summer as they walk through a park. Was it always that way, or have times really changed?

"A Day at the Office" was performed at the 2006 Summer Strawberry One Act Festival and at the Producers Club Theatre. Three business professionals have a "team" meeting to discuss criticism of their project by the big boss. The intensity of the meeting causes each to drift off and individually evaluate the situation.

"Going to Paris" is a short fantasy.

"The Last Word" was performed at the 2008 Summer Strawberry One Act Festival and in 2005 with Love Creek Productions. A young woman laments the paternal restrictions of her youth, attempting to convince her mother that the time has come to make their feelings known. Was it really that bad?

"Daydreams" was performed at the Parker Theatre in 2008. It explores a reason to keep on dreaming.

"A Matter of Choice" depicts a meeting of former lovers that evolves into bitterness as one contemplates the past and the solutions she found.

"The Hired Hand" was a semifinalist at the 2007 Summer Strawberry One Act Festival. A professional woman in her 40s desires to fill her physical needs without the pitfalls of a relationship.

"Diplomacy" is a look into the not-too-distant future. It was performed at the Parker Theatre in 2008.

"The Best of Friends" is a comedy. Men are often accused of thinking with that "other head" of theirs. This play presents such a conversation as the weekend approaches.

"Cross Roads" was performed at the Creative Space Theatre in 2005. It is a play about a choice. A middle-aged man seems lost as he ponders aloud if he has exhausted all the experiences that life has to offer. He gets help in evaluating alternatives.

Dedication

To the family

Kathleen, Marisa, Darren and Cristina

Special thanks to past directors Shawn Madsen and Becky Copley

The Fourth Voice

Time: Now.

Place: A residential bedroom with adjoining bath.

Setting: A woman in her late 20s, Debbie, is looking into a mirror, putting on the final touches of make-up and last-minute accessories for a date that evening. In the background, there is a bed, a dresser, and a small loveseat.

Debbie *(To herself as she looks into the mirror applying mascara.)* There. … That looks good. Well, maybe just a touch more so it stands out a bit. … Okay … done! *(Starts to put away make-up but gives herself a final look over.)* I hope he appreciates all the work I have to put into doing this. Men think you just wake up and look gorgeous. *(Looks at herself again in the mirror.)* But then again, who really cares? … I look good, I know it, and I like it! *(Laughs to herself.)* If I had to rely on a man to fulfill my life, I would still be waiting tables at Bennigan's. *(Stepping back from the mirror to look at herself in full figure and admiring her appearance.)* Eat your heart out, men, this woman can go it alone.

> *(A woman, Voice One, enters from the rear, unseen by Debbie, and sits down on the loveseat as if she is at home.)*

Voice One   Don't be so naïve.

Debbie   *(Turning around.)* You again.

Voice One   Time you settled down and started to get into something serious.

Debbie Why is it that every time I go out on a date you have to come into my head? Can't I just go out and have fun, be catered to … flirt a bit … enjoy myself … then come home and go to sleep. No long-term anything. Just fun.

Voice One Because that's not what you're looking for.

Debbie Oh, I know what I'm looking for … tonight anyway. Just a nice simple evening, no games, no role-play, no one to impress. I'm so sick of playing games all the time. No matter where I am, I always have to make sure I have the right image, say the right things. When I meet people, I have to worry about how I look, what I say, make like I care. I get tired of it. I just want to be me for a few hours.

Voice One Unfortunately, Dear Deborah, one never completely gets away from playing a role and trying to make an impression … especially when you're dating a new guy. Gamesmanship is important if you want to attract a man.

Debbie Again with that. I'm not looking to attract a man.

Voice One *(Playfully.)* Yes you are!

Debbie *(Playfully.)* No I'm not!

Voice One You need a man! It makes no sense to argue about it. Just face up to it. The sooner you do the better off you will be. Then and only then can you live this independent life that you seem to want so badly.

Debbie Independence to me is not waiting on a man hand and foot, making dinner, washing his clothes, keeping his mail straight. Relying on him to do things I can do myself so I can stroke his ego.

Voice One   It's security if you ask me. *(Beat. Changing her tone.)* A nice strong man to walk with at night … to sleep with when it's cold and dark … to move furniture, put up a picture, take out the trash, fix that leak in the basement. It's a small price to pay if you ask me.

Debbie   Yes, yes, I know. You forgot to mention financial and emotional security.

Voice One   Financial and emotional security, of course.

Debbie   Oh, and don't forget companionship and social acceptance.

Voice One   It seems you know that already.

Debbie   How can I not? You constantly bring it up. Look, I have taken pains to make sure I got my education. To make sure I have a job that pays good money—really good money—where I can think, use my brain, and not be treated as some type of inferior sex object. I work hard. I learn more every day just to make enough money so I can have the things I want and not have to rely on anyone, male or female, to get it for me.

Voice One   That's very noble of you. I'm impressed. Fact is it doesn't hurt to have someone do it for you. Share the load every now and then. It is also a fact of life, Dear Deborah, that the older a woman gets the greater her physical needs become and the less likely she will be able to find it. It's unfortunate … it's unfair … but like I said, Dear Deborah, you need a man!

Debbie   Thanks, that is very encouraging, my future as an invalid. *(Beat.)* Sure it helps to have a man around. I don't deny that. Maybe all the things you mentioned are true for some women. Maybe I'll need some of those things myself … who knows? Maybe sometime … but not tonight. Tonight, I want to be me.

Voice One   *(Forcefully.)* You are almost thirty years old and time is a-wasting. Those jeans you have on may not fit you next year, your hair will go gray, you'll have wrinkles in places you never imagined, and your flesh will wobble when you walk.

Debbie   Rush things along, why don't you? I take care of myself. I'll never let myself go. It's part of who I am. *(Continues to dress, trying on shoes.)* I don't like these jeans all that much anyway, but they're good for now. Maybe I'll go shopping tomorrow, get something a little more in style.

Voice One   *(More forcefully.)* Men don't want women who are over the hill.

Debbie   I am far from being over the hill. I'm in my prime if you ask me. *(Proudly.)* I never looked so good.

Voice One   Precisely. That's why you have to make a choice … <u>now …</u> while you still have those looks. *(Circling as if giving instructions.)* One day—and that day will come sooner than you can imagine—you will look in that mirror of yours and you will notice lines in your forehead. Your cheeks will be puffy, your hips will be wide, and your boobs will be sagging. You'll look at that reflection and ask, "Why am I home all alone again?" Then you will see the answer. It will be looking at you!

Debbie   Jesus Christ, will you stop with that? People get older, that's what happens.

Voice One   *(Pleading.)* Deborah, you need to realize that now is the time. Use the time you have or it will become your enemy. We can't go it alone! We were not made to go it alone! What will people say? What would people think?

Debbie   *(Abruptly.)* Get lost!

Voice One   You need a man!

Debbie   <u>Out</u>!

> *(Voice One walks to the back and sits and sulks. Debbie continues dressing, picking out earrings. Unseen by Debbie, a slightly older woman, Voice Two, enters from the back carrying an infant in a blanket.)*

Voice Two   She has a point, you know.

Debbie   *(Recognizing the voice.)* Oh, no. No! No! No!

Voice Two   *(Continuing.)* Although I don't totally agree with her logic. Women have another purpose for wanting a man around. A purpose far more important then money, companionship, or putting out the trash.

Debbie   *(Sarcastically.)* Ms. Motherhood. I should have known. What's on your mind … as if I didn't know. Come on, tell me. Get it over with. See if you can ruin my entire night. Damn! I just want to go out for one night without hearing all these <u>voices</u>.

Voice Two   You should go out and enjoy yourself. Go, have a ball. Who's telling you not to? But it doesn't hurt to look over this guy … uh … what's his name?

Debbie   Dave.

Voice Two   Dave. Look over this guy for long-term potential and try to see what type of a father he will be.

Debbie   You are jumping the gun a bit, don't you think? I just met him a few weeks ago, and I'm already having his child.

Voice Two   Your child!

Debbie   Whatever.

Voice Two   Big difference! Listen, all I'm saying is that you need to keep this in your mind all the time. What happens if you really get attached to this ... this ...

Debbie   Dave.

Voice Two   Dave, and you find out he doesn't want children?

Debbie   This is silly. *(Beat.)* Then I won't marry him.

Voice Two   Then you would have wasted your time.

Debbie   Going out to dinner with an attractive man and having some fun is not wasting my time. *(Beat.)* Besides, I'm not even sure I want kids. *(Voice Two reacts by grabbing her chest in horror.)* All the pain I'll have to go through just giving birth, not to mention changing diapers, getting up in the middle of the night, going to school, the teenage years. Oh my God the teenage years. I wonder how my mother survived. Talk about not having a life of your own. *(Slight laugh to herself.)* Imagine if I had a girl just like me. Oh my God! I'll pull every strand of hair out of my head.

Voice Two   You might at that, but you would love doing it.

Debbie   What exactly does that mean?

Voice Two   It means that you would love to have a girl just like you. *(Hands the baby in the blanket to Debbie, who takes it uncomfortably.)* It means that no matter what she does, no matter how much trouble she can create, no matter if she is pretty or homely, smart or slow, slim or chubby, she is your child. Your child and no one else's. Someone whose entire existence is because of you. Someone who depends on you for nourishment in every sense of the word. Think of how wonderful it would be seeing her growing up, learning, and blossoming into a beautiful woman. Think of how much of you would be in her. Think of all the things you can do through her. Her achievements would be yours ... all the things you never did.

Debbie   All right, stop! You made your point. Becoming a mother is something that I want. You know that. I want that like every other woman on the planet ... but not tonight. I don't want to become a mother tonight. *(Thinking,)* "All the things I never did." You're right! You are absolutely right. There are a lot of things I never did ... and I intend to do them now on my own. Precisely why this "mommy" thing will have to wait a few years or so. How can I teach my child about life if I haven't lived it myself? So go away for a while. Take a rest. See me in a few years. *(Hands the baby back.)*

Voice Two   Your biological clock will be ticking ... ticking. *(With lower volume as Debbie answers.)* Tick tock tick.

Debbie   Well, let it tick loud and fast. Tell me when it's quarter to twelve. I'm going out tonight and having a blast. I might even have sex. Umm, it's been a while, but if things go the right way and if he's not too much of an ass maybe I'll invite him over for a nightcap of sorts.

(Voice Two retreats to the back and sits with Voice One. A woman, Voice Three, enters dressed provocatively in a short skirt and very high heels. She sits down and crosses her legs.)

Voice Three   Now that's more like it.

Debbie   *(Looking over and recognizing Voice Three.)* Oh, it's you. I haven't heard from you for a while.

Voice Three   That's because you're not listening. You're too occupied with that job of yours and those two others back there who only try to inhibit you.

Debbie   So what do you think? Should I?

Voice Three   Should you? What are you waiting for? What has it been, three months? No question in my mind.

Debbie   I don't know. He's still sort of new. *(Beat, modeling her choice of clothes.)* What do you think of my outfit?

Voice Three   Well, if you're looking to get laid tonight, I think you need to spice it up a bit … a whole lot, actually.

Debbie   You have a way with words, I must say. Spice it up? How so?

Voice three   By getting new jeans, for one. You have a nice ass … show it. Don't you have better ones … or maybe a nice short dress?

(Voice Three goes over to a dresser drawer and starts to look through Debbie's clothes and underwear, tossing on the floor the ones that don't fit her style.)

Debbie   These are comfortable.

Voice Three   *(Continuing to go through the drawer.)* Comfort doesn't get you laid. Think of how far that Monica girl got by just flashing her thong.

Debbie   *(Repeatedly picking up clothes from the floor that are being tossed.)* Monica Lewinski? She's a slut.

Voice Three   Maybe so, but she got to suck off the president. Now, how many girls can say that? Talk about using your head. That's feminine power! *(She holds up and admires a brief thong.)*

Debbie   *(Laughing and grabbing the thong away from her.)* You're too much. I'm not going to be flashing my thong or exposing my butt. I don't want him to get the wrong impression.

Voice Three   What impression is that?

Debbie   I don't want him to think I'm too easy.

Voice Three   Forget what he thinks. You've tried this virtuous approach, and all it gets you is ho-hum sex when and if you have it. Just blah! Think about yourself. If you make it too hard or wait until he knows you too well, then any sex you have will be inhibited. It will stay like that forever if you start off too tame. You'll have a personality to protect. Sometimes you want to let it all go … totally unrestrained. Fucking not lovemaking. Having a man totally ravage your body and not being afraid to say, "Fuck me."

Debbie Enough with that type of talk. I don't like it.

Voice Three Oh, yes you do!

Debbie I most certainly do not. I would never talk like that … like I'm making a porno movie. Maybe it's good for the guy, but it doesn't do anything for me.

Voice Three You never tried it.

Debbie And I never will. I don't want to be treated like a whore.

Voice Three Of course not. Not all the time anyway … but every once in a while it doesn't hurt to play around like one. It's an experience. Sounds exciting, now, doesn't it?

Debbie Get real.

Voice Three I am real … very real. *(Beat.)* Think of it, here's a chance to start a relationship like you never have started one before. A chance to live on the wild side. Every woman has a wild side, you know. Most never let go enough to experience it. They protect themselves at all cost, afraid of what it might do to their "golden" reputation.

Debbie My reputation is important.

Voice Three I agree. Reputation is important … but what I'm suggesting is private. Sort of like wearing sexy underwear that no one ever sees nor suspects you have on. No one has to know, just you. You never have to tell a soul.

Debbie I'll know.

Voice Three   Yes, you will, and when you think about it, you'll smile.

Debbie   Or kill myself.

Voice Three   All you are doing is exploring your fantasy … just one time. Like your one-night stand a few years ago.

Debbie   Don't remind me.

Voice Three   It was fun … remember.

Debbie   I'd rather not.

Voice Three   Don't be a tight-ass. Men don't like it.

Voice One   *(Gets up from the back.)* You need to keep men happy.

Voice Two   *(Gets up from the back.)* Find one that's a good father.

Voice One   One that protects you.

Voice Three   One that pleases you.

Voice Two   Your own family.

   (They begin to move around Debbie in a circle as they speak rapidly.)

Voice One   Security and piece of mind.

Voice Three   Hot sex.

Voice Two   A little girl just like you.

Voice One   You don't have to work.

Voice Three   Raw sex.

Voice Two   Picking out her clothes for school.

Voice One   A companion. … A friend.

Voice Three   Just have sex. … Lots of sex.

Voice Two   The holidays. … All the toys.

Voice One   A man!

Voice Three   Two guys. … Maybe three.

Voice Two   Your biological mandate.

(In very rapid succession, closing the circle as they speak.)

Voice One   Protection.

Voice Three   Hot men.

Voice Two   Dolls.

Voice One   Old age.

Voice Three   Fantasyland.

Voice Two   Ribbons and candy.

Voice One   Social acceptance.

Voice Three   Fucking.

Voice Two   Mommy.

Debbie   *(Screaming, causing all three to take a few steps back.)* Ahhhhhhhh! Stop It! Stop it, all of you! I have had enough. On and on and over and over. Again and again. I hear you every moment when I'm alone. Now you need to hear me and hear me loud and clear. *(Beat.)* Sure, I'd like a man, a companion. Sure, I'd like to be a mother and even have a few sexual adventures along the way. But I have to take care of myself and enjoy myself and the life I'm living. I don't exist for the benefit of someone else. I want to experience the things I want to experience where and when I want to experience them.

(Walks around addressing each voice separately.)

When I get up out of my bed every morning and go into <u>my</u> bathroom in <u>my</u> house to get ready to go to <u>my</u> job in <u>my</u> car to make <u>my</u> money to take care of <u>myself</u> ... I feel good. I think ... I've accomplished all this all by my lonesome. That means more to me than having someone hand it to me. Security, protection? Well, living alone has taught me how to fend for myself. Experience is the best teacher. I don't need to rely on some guy with no backbone who probably will run back to his mommy if the going gets tough.

Motherhood ... yes, of course, and I'll cross that bridge when I come to it. Right now I'm still on the road and enjoying the scenery. It's beautiful out there if you stop to look. ... And if it's not meant to be, it's not meant to be. *(Voice Two sighs in horror.)* I'll find the courage to accept it. I have to. I have only one life to live.

If I choose to make love to a man, I'll do it when and however I want. I don't need to play the games that are only of interest to men to satisfy their fantasy so they can get turned on. Hah!

(Addressing all three.)

Do you know what turns me on? Do you? *(Beat.)* My turn-on, ladies, is <u>me</u>. That's all. Just little ole me. That's my turn-on, and you know it happens every single day. Every day I look at myself and say, "Go for it, Deborah." Yes, it takes some convincing at times because I keep hearing all these voices preaching compromising alternatives. In the end, I listen to that voice inside me that gives me the courage to press on and enjoy whatever comes my way. Whatever it is and whatever it takes, I'll handle it.

(Looking at her watch to check if she is running late, then pausing to think.)

You know … I'm going to cancel tonight. I'm really not in the mood anymore, so why bother. *(Beat.)* Instead … maybe I'll call Lisa; she's been asking me for months to stop over. I haven't seen her in a long time. Umm, let me check.

(Picks up her cell phone and dials.)

Voice Three   What are you doing?

Voice One   Don't be silly.

Voice Two   Put that phone down.

Debbie   Shut up! *(Into the phone.)* Hi Lisa. Deborah. You gonna be home tonight? … Great. … No, nothing's up. I

just need a change from the rat race. ... Pizza is fine. I'll
bring some wine. ... In about a half hour. ... Great. See you
soon. ... Oh! Call Kate and see if she wants to stop by. Bye.

(Debbie gathers up her purse and keys.)

Debbie   So, ladies, there you have it. I've heard your pleas
and it was good we talked, but for tonight ... I'm going to
have a ball.

(Debbie exits. The others sit down in frustration.)

Voice Two   Could you beat that?

Voice One   What nerve.

Voice Three   Boring.

End.

Changing Times

Time: An early summer evening.

Place: A park.

Setting: A married couple in their early 50s, Jay and Jane, are walking in a neighborhood park on a beautiful warm early summer evening. In the foreground are assorted flowers and shrubbery and a park bench. Walking by at various times are men, women, children, and couples walking hand in hand admiring the scenery.

Jay Ah! What a nice night. *(Takes a deep breath in.)* Just beautiful. Let's take a break and find a place to sit … look out over the water for a bit … smell the ocean.

Jane Now? Not right now. I'm a little tired, and I've got things to do. Besides, the water smells funky, and we have to get back to let the dog out.

Jay The water doesn't smell funky. It smells like an ocean should smell. And the dog will be fine. It'll be good to relax a bit.

Jane No time to relax. *(Jay gives her a look, which she recognizes.)* All right. Not too long, though.

Jay Here, this bench has a good view.

(Walking over and sitting on the bench.)

Jane These old park benches are so uncomfortable. You'd think they would have come up with something better by now.

Jay What do you expect, cushions? Some things never change. Relax. It's not like we're going to sit here for hours. Just a few minutes.

Jane *(Uncomfortable and twitching in her seat.)* These park benches make me feel like I'm on display. So open. Everyone who passes by looks at you.

Jay And we look at everyone who passes by. That's part of the fun.

Jane It is? Not for me. I don't need to be examined by the world. *(Beat.)* I never really liked these benches.

Jay *(Admiring the view.)* This is nice. I'm so glad it's summer.

Jane Hope it doesn't get as hot as last year. You couldn't even breathe outside, it was so humid. Then every weekend—without fail—rain.

Jay That was last year. Enjoy the moments while you can.

Jane It won't last. I know it. *(Beat. Sitting back a bit and relaxing, albeit reluctantly.)* It is sort of nice out now. The water is so blue … like a crayon. Bet it's ice cold.

Jay Sure it is. That's why we're looking at it and not swimming in it.

Jane Swimming, I don't think anything could be alive in there. It has to be filthy.

Jay No, I think they keep it rather clean.

Jane *(Recollecting.)* I haven't been to the ocean swimming for years. I can't even remember the last time.

Jay It's been a while. Several years, at that. You used to love the water and the beach. What happened?

Jane I did once. Now it's just such a hassle to get there and back … and from what I hear they are always packed. If I want to get some sun, I'll sit out in my own backyard where it's private and I'm more comfortable. I don't need all that dirty sand all over me. Besides, I never know what type of suit to wear. All the suits I have are ancient, and … I'm not twenty years old anymore. The beach is for the young.

Jay It is? When did they pass that law?

(A young couple holding hands walk by and then stop to admire the view. They kiss softly and then again more passionately. Jane takes notice and is uncomfortable and annoyed.)

Jane Looks like we got some lovebirds.

Jay *(Not noticing until they are mentioned.)* What? Oh! Just kids.

(The kissing becomes more passionate. Jane becomes more uncomfortable and seemingly horrified as she stares at the couple with her mouth open. Jay does not take notice.)

Jane My God, will you look at that? He's all over her. Can't they wait until they get home?

Jay *(Looking over.)* What? Oh? Why are you staring at

them? They probably don't have a place of their own to go to. You got to admit, it's a nice spot to steal a kiss or two.

Jane   A kiss or two? A kiss or two is fine, but he practically has his hands in her pants. I'm going to tell them to move. *(Attempts to get up.)* Excuse …

Jay   *(Stopping her.)* Sit. They are not bothering anyone.

Jane   They are bothering me. I don't want to have to watch that.

Jay   So don't.

Jane   How can I not? *(Continuing to stare.)* My God, look how she's dressed. Those jeans are so low-cut you could see her underwear … or her thong … what little there is to it.

Jay   *(Abruptly stretching his neck playfully to get a better look.)* What! Where? I love it!

(People pass by.)

Jane   Stop, people are watching you. *(Giving him a shove back into the seat.)* I don't know, maybe it's me, but I can't see why any self-respecting female would want to show her underwear in public. *(Shakes her head.)* When I was a young girl, we would have to wear a slip under our dresses so no one could see underneath or through the material.

Jay   A slip? Do they still make those?

Jane   *(Ignoring him.)* In fact, my mother made sure that when I went out I wore a top that hid my bra. Now every girl you see has to flash her underwear. Let everyone see how skimpy it could be. Thongs, no less, how uncomfortable. Why wear anything? Just show your ass ... and the tops they wear ... gracious ... why not just take them out?

Jay   Why not is right.

Jane   *(Ignoring him.)* The new thing now is tattoos. Big ugly tattoos right over their butt or on their boobs. So stupid. What are they going to do with that tattoo when they're forty years old and their body sags and wrinkles. It will look like shit. Faded images of garbage and names of former boyfriends who left you cold.

Jay   Lighten up. If you remember, you did things like that too way back when.

Jane   I most certainly did not!

Jay   You did so. I was there, remember?

Jane   I don't have any tattoos, and I for sure never walked around in public with my underwear showing!

Jay   That's because sometimes you didn't wear any.

Jane   What?

Jay   What was that look back then? I think it was called "going braless."

Jane   *(Acknowledging, but somewhat embarrassed.)* Well, I was young back then. We all did it to go with the style.

Jay   My point exactly! You can't judge these kids nowadays until you remember the things you did yourself back then.

Each generation has its own way of exploring itself.

Jane   That's true, I understand, but you have to draw the line somewhere. I mean, how far can you go? Should it be okay to walk in the streets naked? *(Beat.)* Braless … I haven't heard that term in years. What was I thinking back then?

Jay   You weren't.

> *(The young couple give each other one final embrace and then exit. Jane watches as they leave.)*

Jane   Good, they finally left. I though for a while we were going to have live porn.

Jay   Now, that would be worthy of my attention. Janey, they were just kissing.

Jane   I suppose.

> *(Jay puts his arm around Jane.)*

Jay   Look at that sky, that red glow. It's beautiful. Sort of romantic out here tonight. *(He pulls her closer.)*

Jane   *(Uncomfortable, moving away.)* Okay, let's get back.

Jay   No, let's stay a while. What are we going to do back home anyway?

Jane   I've got plenty of things I have to … *(Jay pulls her closer and kisses her on the forehead.)* do before it gets. … Will you stop that? (*She pulls his hand off her back.)* The whole park is watching. What if someone we know sees us?

Jay   What if they do?

Jane   I'd feel like an idiot that's what.

Jay   Oh, come on.

(He kisses her on the lips and she fights him off.)

Jane   I said not here!

Jay   Why not?

Jane   Because I'm not going to be seen making out on a park bench. I'll look so dumb. People would say, "Did you see that old woman and guy making out on the bench?" My God, I'd be mortified.

Jay   Who cares what they say if you never hear it?

Jane   I can only imagine. *(He comes closer again, a bit more forcefully.)* No, I said! I am not into kissing on a park bench in the middle of the day with thousands of people around me.

Jay   We did when we were younger.

Jane   That was different.

Jay   Why should it be different?

Jane   Because it was. *(Beat.)* Even back then, whenever we did anything, we always used your car and went parking at night, so at least we had some privacy.

Jay   The '64 Chevy. I loved that car.

Jane   What a jalopy that was. Although it was pretty roomy … well, not really, but it's all we had.

Jay   It was fun. We had some good times in there.

Jane   Oh my God, don't remind me. Talk about wild oats.

Jay   It was wild at that. The parking lot was loaded with cars. I remember, whenever someone came into the lot they would turn off their headlights as soon as they entered. Parking lot etiquette. All the kids were doing the same thing.

Jane   It was the only place we had. Both our parents were home all the time.

Jay   Remember, sometimes the cops would come by and shine their flashlights in the window.

Jane   How could I forget? I'd be half-dressed and all of a sudden there's this light shining right in my eyes. So embarrassing. The cops must have had a good time.

Jay   They did! So did we.

Jane   Yes we did.

Jay   Remember the snowstorm?

Jane   I sure do. We laid down in the back, and the next time we looked up there was a foot of snow on the ground.

Jay   You couldn't even see out the window. Just the faint glow of the streetlight, and so, so quiet. … Not a sound.

Jane   We almost had to spend the night there, and all we had was an old army blanket. We would have froze.

Jay Funny, I don't remember feeling cold.

Jane No. As a matter of fact, it was nice and warm ... sort of cozy.

> *(Jay moves closer and attempts to kiss Jane again. She again stops him.)*

Jane But that was then, and this is now. We are not teenagers anymore, and I'm not making out on a park bench.

Jay I'm not looking to make out, just a kiss. ... You're getting old.

Jane I am old, and times have changed. We have a house with a bed and heat. Seems like a more appropriate place, don't you think?

Jay Ho-hum.

Jane Ho-hum nothing. Act your age.

Jay I do, all the time. That's the problem.

Jane Well, times have changed, and you have to recognize that. We've changed. C'mon, lets go.

Jay No, not yet. *(Beat.)* Why is that?

Jane Why is what?

Jay Why do times change? Why do we have to change? Have we? I mean, I'm still the same person I always was. So are you.

Jane   Except that what's left of your hair is all gray, your waistline is forty inches, and your muscles are sagging. I'm a size ten, with thinning hair, and going through menopause. Need any more reasons?

Jay   I don't feel older … well, somewhat … but not <u>old</u> or <u>different</u>. When I look in the mirror, I still see myself. The same guy I've been talking to for fifty years. I still like the same things. I still like to do the same things I did years ago. I don't think I've changed all that much. I'm smarter and wiser, that's for sure, and I have put on a few pounds, but I don't feel that I've really changed. *(Beat.)* Let me ask you a question.

Jane   Go ahead.

Jay   What was it that really bothered you about that couple that was here before?

Jane   The lovebirds?

Jay   Yes.

Jane   I think there is a time and place for everything.

Jay   Do you? Did you always?

Jane   I don't know about always, but I do now.

Jay   What about the beach? Why is it that you don't want to go?

Jane   I told you.

Jay   How about sitting on this bench … right here in front of the world? Why does that bother you? Why do you care what that girl was wearing or if her underwear was showing or that they were embracing?

Jane I told you.

Jay You told me, but that's not the real answer.

Jane It's not?

Jay No!

Jane Then what is it then? You seem to know so much.

Jay I think the real answer is that ... you're jealous.

Jane What?

Jay I mean, what you are seeing—what they are doing— are all things that you once loved to do and that you would still love to do but don't because society tells you—tells us— we can't ... we are too old. When we see a couple kissing or walking hand in hand on the beach or just watching the sunset over the water, we say to ourselves, "I wish I could do that." We have become so self-conscious about our age that it stops us from doing what we like. It doesn't have to be like that. It shouldn't be like that. Age changes us physically, but it doesn't have to change us unless we let it. Sure, youth has its beauty, its virility, its excitement, but you know what? You were beautiful and exciting back then, ... And you know what? You still are. Don't lose it.

Jane *(Smiling.)* Thanks, that was nice of you. I think I needed that.

(She leans over and gives him a big kiss.)

Jay   There! You see, that wasn't all that bad, now, was it?

Jane   No, it was sort of nice. I'm glad I married such a smart man.

Jay   I'm glad you did too.

(He leans over and tries to kiss her again. She just gives him a peck and pushes him back.)

Jane   *(Playfully.)* All right. Let's not push it. Time to go.

(She gets up.)

Jay   I can't win.

(She offers her hand to help him up.)

Jane   You just did.

Jay   Really, how so?

Jane   Oh, I don't know. No one is home right now, and we have that loveseat swing in the backyard, and like you said, it is a nice night … maybe some wine and, hey, you never can tell.

Jay   That's my girl!

(They exit hand in hand.)

End.

A Day at the Office

Time: Now.

Place: An office anywhere in the United States.

Setting: A department manager (Bob) is sitting alone in his office working at a computer. Bob is in his early 40s and dressed in a shirt and tie. In the office there are a desk, three chairs, a small conference table, a telephone, and the usual array of office supplies. A secretary (Sophie, 30s, average in all respects) walks into Bob's office.

Sophie *(Handing Bob a report with noticeable red marks on it.)* John said he wants to talk to you about this "first thing in the morning."

Bob *(Taking the report with worry.)* Tomorrow? Did he say anything?

Sophie Oh, yeah! He had lots of things to say. I couldn't make out most of it. I think you will hear about it tomorrow.

Bob What do you mean?

Sophie He mumbled something about teamwork and putting together a professional package and … ah, you know how he gets. You'll need to read it all.

Bob *(Glancing at the report.)* Oh shit! Was he pissed?

Sophie Don't know.

Bob Well, what do you think?

Sophie *(Smiles.)* I'm not paid enough to think. Tomorrow, first thing.

(She starts to walk out.)

Bob Wait a second … should I bring Janet and Mike?

Sophie I have no idea.

Bob Well, did he say anything else?

Sophie I don't remember.

(She leaves.)

Bob *(To himself, very annoyed.)* Not paid to think. That's because you can't … useless bitch. *(Looking at the report.)* Damn. I knew I should have changed that. *(Paging through, talking to himself under his breath.)* Picky bastard. … Now, that don't make sense. I told her not to put that in. … Damn her. *(Picking up the phone.)* Mike, get Janet and come into my office. It's about the Phillips account. … No, now!

(He hangs up and paces around the office nervously.)

Bob *(To himself, under his breath.)* Shit, I knew I shouldn't have volunteered. I really don't need this. Not again. Now I have to come up with reasons. I'm not going to take all the heat myself, not this time. *(Shakes his head in silence.)*

(Janet and Mike enter.)

(Mike is about 25 years old, dressed in a shirt and tie and looking very professional. Janet is in her mid-20s, has long hair, and is dressed in a loose-fitting

top, a skirt, and heels. Her appearance is businesslike but still fashionable and attractive.)

Mike   Hey boss, what's up?

Janet   Hey, Bob.

Bob   Have a seat, guys.

(They sit around a small conference table.)

Mike   *(Noticing the report in Bob's hand.)* So I see John had some comments.

Bob   To say the least.

Mike   Did you talk to him about it?

Bob   No, I just got his comments from Sophie.

Mike   What did she say?

Bob   Nothing. She's too stupid to know what is going on.

Mike   I thought you were going to talk to John beforehand … sort of grease the skids. Explain why we chose to use the approach we did. Makes it easier to understand.

Bob   I didn't have the time.

Mike   You should have told me. I would have talked to him.

Bob   *(Angrily.)* A report that comes out of my staff has to be able to stand on its own.

Mike But, Boss, that was the whole idea. It was your suggestion.

Bob I didn't! Enough said!

Janet I thought we took a good approach … pretty unique.

Bob I thought so too, but you know John.

Janet He's not very open-minded, but I thought even <u>he</u> would like this one.

Bob Well, apparently he did not! Now I have to go in there tomorrow and give him reasons … and I'm on his shit list right now. I can't get any deeper into the shit than I am right now. He's going to tell me, "I have a responsibility to the company." … "I have to make sure things are done right and that the people I work with are capable of living up to his standards." And all the other stuff. Damn! *(Beat.)* Mike, I'm really disappointed with you on this.

Mike Me?

Janet Was it that bad?

Mike I thought it was good. What didn't he like?

Bob I don't know exactly. I haven't read through everything, but judging from all these red marks, he apparently was not satisfied. I'm surprised I got it back in one piece. Now he's on this teamwork kick. That's his new thing. He's big on it. I think he is disappointed with as us as a team. He's made several comments to me about dedication and working together.

Janet You're absolutely right, he loves to preach about teamwork. But he shouldn't have an issue with this. We did work on it together. I put a lot of time into it myself, *(To Bob.)* added your suggestions, which by the way I thought were terrific. *(Crosses her legs.)* I don't think John appreciates your creativity and ability.

Bob I know, Jan. Thanks! I know you added a lot yourself, and your work was the best part of the presentation. If it wasn't for you, it never would have gotten this far. I'll be sure to mention that to John tomorrow.

Janet *(Shaking her head.)* You added a lot yourself. I just followed your lead. *(Beat.)* You know, I'm pissed. He doesn't appreciate you. ... What would he do without you? You work harder than anyone here and have been here the longest. It's just not fair.

Bob Thanks.

Janet You are so creative. Guess there's no room for that in this organization.

Mike We all worked on it. I came in Saturday to do some research and piece everything together. Took me all day.

Bob You did?

Mike Yes I did!

Janet I was going to come in too.

Mike I thought you were coming in. I was expecting you.

Janet I was. I just got sidetracked and before I knew it, it was late, and then it was such a nice day. ... I had so many things I had to catch up on. I figured, when am I going to find the time? I went shopping, got everything out of the way. Anyway, I thought you could handle most of it by yourself.

Bob   I was going to come in also, but ended up playing golf. Just to get my senses back. I think we both needed a break.

Mike   *(Sarcastically.)* Why do you think he has a problem with teamwork?

Bob   He wants to see that everyone is involved.

Mike   Well, each of us signed the report.

Bob   *(Looking away.)* Not exactly. *(Beat.)* It only had my signature on it. *(Mike looks at Bob with disbelief.)* I had to change something on the last page and neither of you were around, so I did what I had to do. Besides, I didn't want you to take the heat.

Mike   So he doesn't think we worked on it.

Bob   He will tomorrow. I'll be sure to tell him you were the project leader on this one and that I gave you full control.

Mike   Thanks a lot.

Bob   He wanted me to delegate more down to you … and so I did. I told him you may not be ready.

Mike   I think if I talk to him, I could explain it.

Bob   I'll talk to him first. Then, if he wants, you can make your case. What I want you to do right now is to look over all these comments and have some answers for me <u>tonight</u> so

I can read them in the morning. I'll have Sophie make some copies. *(Picks up the phone.)* Sophie, can you come in here for a minute?

Mike Tonight? I'm supposed to have dinner with the McBride account at their country club.

Bob You'll have plenty of time to catch up with the McBrides. Janet and I will go in your place. Are you free, Jan?

Janet Tonight ... oh, well ... yes. I'd love to go. ... If it's okay with Mike?

Mike That's my favorite project. I've been looking forward to ...

Bob You have work to do. Besides, I want the McBrides to meet Janet. It'll be good for her.

Janet I don't know anything about the account. I just talked to him once on the phone.

Bob Don't worry. I'll tell you all you need to know.

Janet I'll have to go home and change.

Bob Well, that's up to you, but I think you look fine. I love that outfit, by the way.

Janet Thanks, it's just something I threw on.

Bob Looks nice, but if you need an hour or so, that will be okay. Mike, what time does it start?

Mike Six ... I think.

Bob Don't think! Find out for sure, and give Jan the directions.

Janet Sorry, Mike. *(Pats him on the hand.)* I'll be sure to mention your name.

Mike Thanks a lot.

(Sophie enters.)

Bob *(To Sophie, handing her the report.)* Do you think you can make two copies for Mike and Janet?

Sophie *(Sarcastically.)* I'm not sure. There are so many buttons. Just two copies?

Bob I think that's what I said. Didn't I say two, Janet?

Janet Two.

Sophie Two copies or two copies each?

Bob Now, does it make sense to make two copies each?

Sophie You need to be specific.

Bob Two! Is that clear? Just two.

(Sophie leaves.)

Janet *(Laughing.)* Did you say two?

Bob My God! Is she dense? A bowling ball has more sense.

Janet   She's not the brightest light.

Bob   Light, I'm talking blackout. *(They both laugh. Mike smiles faintly.)* Mike, listen to me, you need to get your priorities straight ... and fast. Work comes first. I won't accept anything else. I broke my back to get to where I am. If you expect me to keep pulling you along, you are sadly mistaken. This project is yours so face up to it.

Mike   I know it was mine, but I ran everything through you. You signed off on it. You said you liked ...

Bob   STOP! In the first place, I signed off because I had to show John something ... something to show for the last three weeks. Secondly, I thought you were going to present it differently. I can't check every little detail. *(Beat.)* Mike, we are a team and I am the leader ... you are a player. I give my team enormous flexibility in doing their job. That's just how I am. I need dedication. That's all I ask. If something goes wrong, I take the heat ... and I don't like heat! When I was your age, why, I put in twenty hours a day, seven days a week, twelve months a year. Took work home every night, worked till two in the morning. No vacations, no gourmet meals. *(Beat.)* I had little kids at home and my wife didn't like it one bit ... not one bit. She divorced me because of it. So I've sacrificed a lot. Put all I had into this job and this company. I have to maintain ...

> *(The action freezes. Mike gets up and moves to the center of the stage.)*

Mike   *(To the audience.)* Here we go again. The same old history of his glory days. Does he really think I give a shit? "Glory days." Hah! I bet he was a scumbag back then too. He thinks he impresses me with all this dedication and commitment to "the job." He let his whole life slip away to make a few bucks. His wife left him for another man and took everything but his TV. Even now he has nothing except this "job." That won't happen to me. No way! *(Beat. Looking over at Janet.)* Janet is another one. Doesn't do a thing except sit there, look pretty, and stroke the boss's ego. "Yes Bob." "Good idea Bob." "You're absolutely right Bob." Can't blame her, really. She uses the only asset she has, and why not? *(Laughs.)* Wonder if she realizes that all he wants is to get in her pants. *(Beat.)* Office games. Holy shit, I am so sick of all these fucking games that I have to play every single day … day in, day out. He thinks I really care about this teamwork bullshit. What a joke. Everyone here is out for themselves … ourselves. I'm no different. I'm out to find a "godfather" that will pull me along … and it's sure not pathetic Bob. Money, that's all that matters. I have to eat, pay the rent, put gas in the car, and every once in a while impress my female friends with something other than a cheeseburger. MONEY. That's it. That's the name of the game. The rest is crap. Why else would anyone put up with such nonsense? *(Pause.)* Oh, well, let me get back before he notices I've drifted away.

(Mike returns to the table and the action resumes.)

Bob *(Continuing.)* … my reputation for quality and management and focus on the company's goals and objective so that we all can get ahead. When the company makes money, we make money.

Mike Enough! You made your point. I'll get it done.

Bob You bet you will.

Janet Do you want any help? I don't really have to go to dinner tonight.

Bob   Nonsense, I want you to come. Mike needs to focus.

Janet   Are you sure?

Mike   I'll be all right. Keep your cell phone handy. I may call you on some of the points you worked on.

Janet   Will do. What's the big guy's first name?

Mike   Michael.

Janet   Oh, like you. I have to remember.

Mike   Yeah, they call him "Big Mike." He's a nice guy ... has a ton of money. *(Janet begins to drift off in her thoughts.)* I'd like to live in his spare room. You should see his place. He and his brother started up the business in his backyard ...

   (The action freezes. Janet gets up and moves to the center of the stage.)

Janet   *(To the audience.)* "Big Mike." ... Umm, I wonder what he looks like. Anyone with "Big" for a nickname has got to be terrific. He's rich, too ... umm. I'll have to go home and put something really nice on ... my blue pantsuit and a white top ... no ... too formal. I need some color ... my red print blouse and black skirt ... or maybe all black ... much more elegant. I'll wear my black spike heels ... no, that's too much. I'll see when I get home. I've got to get out of here ... fix my hair. Maybe I'll wear it down. Do my nails. *(Looks at her watch and then over at Bob.)* I have to get him to shut up so I can leave. I hope he's not going to be all over me tonight, showing me around like a trophy. I'll need to get off by myself so I can talk one on one with "Big Mike." I can put up with Bob here because I have to, but "Big Mike" is the prize I want. He has

45

money. He has power. He has what I want. *(Beat.)* I'm going to call him Michael or Mr. McBride ... not Mike. Give him an opportunity to introduce informality. Men like that. *(Looking over at the table again.)* I sort of feel sorry for my Mike. He has to put up with all Bob's bull crap. He puts so much into everything he does. How unfortunate. He should have been a woman so he wouldn't have to. *(Beat.)* Let me get back to the lecture. *(Walking back to the table.)* Maybe my new jeans with heels? That might be really nice and different ... sexy.

(Janet returns to the table and the action resumes.)

Mike   *(Continuing.)* ... from scratch, not more than three years ago.

Bob   Hard work has its rewards. *(He notices Janet.)* Jan. ... Janet. ... Are you still with us?

Janet   *(Surprised.)* Oh ... ah ... yes. I was just thinking about a better way to make our case. Should we shorten it a little?

Bob   It's too short as it is.

Janet   Maybe cut out some charts.

Bob   The charts have all the information.

Janet   They do, you're right. I should have remembered that. I'm just pissed about the whole situation and ...

(The action freezes and Bob approaches the audience.)

Bob *(To the audience.)* Jeez, she doesn't have a clue. She has so many loose screws in her head I can hear them jingle. *(Looking at Janet sitting with her legs crossed.)* But she does have legs. I love when she crosses them. *(Beat.)* I think I have a shot with her. She likes me, I'm sure of that. I've got to make my move … maybe tonight. Get her a little bit drunk, say some nice things. She already knows how smart I am. *(Beat.)* It is risky though. My God, I hope she's not a big mouth. It'll be all over for me. Everyone in the office will know. *(Beat.)* Then I'll simply deny it. How's she gonna prove it? It's my word over hers. Who are they gonna believe? I just have to pick the right spot … leave early. There's a Marriott down the street. *(Looking over at the table.)* She is lovely. I'd like to fuck her right here on the table. *(Smiles but then quickly changes to worry as he looks at Mike.)* Mike! I'm worried about him. He's not the sap I thought he was. He is after my job, that bastard. I can't have that. I've got no place to go. Never going to make this type of money. … I have to keep him away from John. Get him to quit … really piss him off … cut his bonus. *(Beat.)* He does do all the work, though. Jan doesn't even understand what he's doing. If I lose him, I'll be cutting off my legs and be up shit creek. I have got to think about something more subtle … some little thing that will poison John's opinion of him. Umm … let me get back.

(Bob returns to the table and the action resumes.)

Janet *(Continuing.)* … all John's comments.

Mike I'm curious about exactly what John said.

(Sophie enters with copies.)

Sophie Well, you can ask him yourself. He's headed down this way.

Bob   Damn it. *(Snatching the report out of Sophie's hand.)* Let me see that fucking thing.

(Janet walks over to look at the report with Bob.)

(John enters.)

Mike   Hey, John.

Janet   John.

Bob   *(A bit nervous.)* We were just going over your comments. We'll have something for you first thing. We'll put our heads together and get this in better shape. I told Mike what I think it needed.

John   Oh, really? What was that?

Bob   Ah, ah … like the charts … I was thinking maybe we should cut out some of them?

John   No. The charts are key. They bring home the points really well. Tie everything together. That's what I liked about it. Very novel approach to overlay them the way you did. It was one of the better products to come out of your group in some time.

Bob   *(Surprised.)* You liked it?

John   Yes, of course I liked it. Didn't you read my summary comment at the end?

Bob   I just glanced at it and saw all these red marks and …

John   Oh, don't mind that. That's the only pen I had. I don't have any real issues, just format things to consider. Overall, it was really good. I was going to tell you that tomorrow, but I thought you'd like to hear it directly from me before you all went home tonight and since you're all together and you are a team.

Bob   Thanks. … We worked hard on it.

Janet   You can say that again.

John   I know I saw Mike here this weekend. *(To Mike.)* Did my suggestions help you any?

Mike   Actually, they did.

John   Good. See, the old dog still knows some tricks. … I didn't see anyone else here Saturday. Did you guys come in too?

Bob   No, I couldn't make it … family problems.

Janet   I had to take my dogs to the vet.

Bob   We were all in early Monday. To see how Mike made out.

John   I see. … Who was the project leader?

Bob   Well … we all worked on it … but Mike sort of took the lead … after we talked over strategy, of course.

John   Of course. *(Beat.)* Mike, have a good time with the McBrides tonight. Tell Big Mike to call me when he wants to go fishing.

Mike   I didn't know you like to fish.

John   Like it? I love it. Haven't you seen the collection I have in my office?

Mike   I've just glanced at them. I didn't think they were real.

John   Not real? *(Puts his arm around Mike.)* My boy, everything is real. Come with me for a few minutes, I'll give you the five-minute tour. Do you do any fishing yourself?

Mike   Some.

John   You need to come out on my boat someday, and I'll …

  (They leave.)

  (Bob and Janet stand alone.)

Bob   Five-minute tour. He'll be there for an hour.

Janet   So, does this mean I can't go to the country club tonight?

  (He gives her a look.)

  (The lights fade.)

End.

Going to Paris

Setting: A man wanders alone around a dimly lit and foggy stage. From the background a man appears in the uniform of a train conductor.

Conductor   All aboard.

Man   What? *(He looks back.)*

Conductor   All aboard.

Man   Who are you?

Conductor   Last call. All aboard!

Man   *(Laughing to himself.)* What are you talking about?

Conductor   Ticket sir.

Man   This is not Grand Central Station. There are no trains here. There are not even any tracks.

Conductor   You need a ticket, sir.

Man   Ticket to where? Where am I going?

Conductor   I can't answer that, sir.

Man   No, of course you can't.

(A woman approaches. She opens her purse and produces two tickets.)

Woman   Is this the train to Paris?

Conductor   It most certainly is.

Woman   Here. *(She hands him the two tickets.)*

Conductor   Expecting someone?

Woman   Yes.

Conductor   *(Giving back the extra ticket.)* Hold onto it for now. We will be leaving shortly.

Man   *(Totally not understanding.)* Pardon me, ma'am, did you say Paris? The train to Paris?

Woman   Yes. Are you going to Paris?

Man   Trains don't go to Paris, Miss. There is a little body of water between here and there. It's called the Atlantic Ocean.

Woman   Oh, just geography. I don't worry about the geography.

Man   Seems like an issue, wouldn't you say?

Woman   Not at all.

Conductor   Five minutes, ma'am.

Woman   I was just trying to help my friend here. He seems a bit lost. Where do I sit?

Conductor   Anywhere you like. Find the place that is most appealing.

Woman   How long is the trip?

Conductor   I can't say for sure, but it's never an issue. We've never had any complaints from those who come along. Sounds like this is your first trip, ma'am.

Woman   No, I've been there before, but that was a long time ago. A very long time ago. I just never was able to get back. I almost forgot how to get there.

Conductor   Getting there is sometimes difficult. I can tell you that. But once you get there, you find it hasn't changed. That's part of the charm of going to Paris. The trip is always different, but the place is undeniable.

Man   *(Who has been observing.)* Oh, come on, you two. Are you actors doing a candid camera skit?

Conductor   Actors, sir?

Man   Yes. What is this nonsense, a train to Paris in the middle of nowhere?

Conductor   Ever been to Paris, sir?

Man   Have I ever been to Paris? ... Yes, as a matter of fact, yes. Several times on business, and I seem to remember one hell of a long flight, bad food, long days, and rain.

Conductor   Then you have obviously never been to Paris.

Man   I just told you I was.

Conductor   I heard you. But I think you may have been mistaken, sir.

Man   The Louvre, the Eiffel Tower, parle vous français?

Conductor   Oui, je parle français.

Man   What?

Conductor   You asked if I spoke French.

Man   No. … I didn't mean that. I was telling you all the sites in Paris.

Conductor   Sites, sir? *(Beat.)* Sir, I suspect you have yet to go to Paris.

Man   What?

Conductor   Sir, there is not a lot of time left. Talk to this lady, she was there some time ago.

(The conductor gathers his belongs and makes one more call.)

Conductor   *(Continued.)* Final call for Paris. Paris final call. *(Fading sounds.)* Final call for Paris.

Man   *(Shaking his head and looking at the woman.)* What a strange man. Can you believe that he had the nerve to tell me that I've never been where I know I have. Paris. April, 1989, I remember I was on business and it rained every day. I remember tha—

Woman   *(Interrupting.)* It doesn't rain in Paris.

Man   It did when I was there. I got soaked. I had forgotten my umbrella in the taxi and …

Woman *(Again interrupting.)* Then you were somewhere else.

Man I was so there. I may have been alone, but I was there.

Woman Most people don't go to Paris alone.

Man Is that some sort of new rule?

Woman There are no rules.

Man You're going alone, are you not?

Woman No, I'm meeting someone.

Man Suppose he—I assume it's a he—doesn't come?

Woman He will.

Man Why can't you go alone?

Woman I hear it's possible, but not for me. I tried for years, but it didn't work.

Man Look, Miss, I'm confused. What is all the mystery going on here? Tell me … tell me all about this Paris that I supposedly have never been to.

Woman Paris, my friend, is like no other place. You'll know it when you get there.

Man You were there, I take it.

Woman Heavens, yes. A long time ago. I would go all the time back then. It was easy back then.

Man   It sure was cheaper. Why haven't you gone back?

Woman   No one to share it with.

Man   Who did you go with when you did go?

Woman   A friend, a companion ... a very good friend.

Man   Where is he now?

Woman   Somewhere else. Life changes people. People are infected by everything around them. There are worries and pain and sickness and responsibility. Misunderstandings, insults, and sins of the flesh. People grow apart. Replacement is difficult.

Man   I can relate to that. Do you know I almost got married once? It was a while ago. I was twenty-six years old. Just starting out in business, Very energetic and driven. I met this woman ... Joanne. That was her name. Joanne. She was about my age. She was beautiful, as most women are at that age, but hers was beyond anything physical. There was something very alluring about her entire being. Calming, peaceful. There were times when I was with her that I almost stopped worrying about business, who I had to call, and how much money I had to make.

Woman   Almost?

Man   Yes, almost. I could never pull away. Joanne tried her best ... begged me to step away. I was selfish, I guess. We broke up ... lost contact. Been totally ingrained in my work ever since.

Woman   Almost.

(He gives a questioning look.)

Woman You were almost there.

Man Where?

Woman Paris.

Man Really. … Tell me about Paris. You've been there. You know all about it.

Woman Paris. … Paris is the smell of coffee in the morning and the first taste of a warm buttered roll. It is the beach in the summer and a blanket in the winter. It is where every touch is as invigorating as it is soothing. It is the glory of the sunrise, the glow of a fireplace, and the smell of a rose. It is being one with the one you are with and being fully confident of each other's contentment. It is love and affection forming the essence of human bonding. What we strive to experience.

Man Sounds like the place to be.

Woman It is. *(Beat.)* Come with me.

(She offers him a ticket. The man takes it but stops.)

Man *(Holding the ticket.)* No, I don't have the money for the ticket, and I don't have the time for such a long trip.

Woman The good thing about going to Paris is that it won't cost you anything, and it doesn't take any time to get there, but you will always remember the being there.

(The conductor returns.)

Conductor   All aboard!

(He takes the ticket and hands it to the conductor.)

(They begin to exit.)

Man   What did you say your name was?

Woman   Joanne.

(They exit, leaving the conductor alone on the stage with a smile on his face.)

End.

The Last Word

Time: Now.

Place: Miami, Florida, on a hot sunny Sunday morning around 11:00 AM.

Setting: The interior of a modestly furnished apartment. A woman in her late 40s (Rosa) is alone meticulously ironing and folding clothing (primarily male). There is a couch, a chair, and a table on which sit a small fan and a bottle of water. The woman is dressed in a loose-fitting housedress but is not in any way sloppy or unattractive.

> *(After a moment a knock is heard on the door.)*

Rosa   Who is it?

Maria   It's me, Momma.

Rosa   Come in, the door is open.

> *(Maria is a young, attractive, and stylish woman in her late 20s dressed fashionably in a short sundress, sunglasses, and low-heeled pumps.)*

Maria   Hi, Momma. *(They hug and kiss on the cheek.)*

Rosa   Since when do you knock? You usually just walk in.

Maria   Well, I don't want to just barge in. Maybe you're in the middle of something special … you know.

Rosa   In the middle of the day? You're funny.

Maria   I've heard about you empty nesters. Where is Dad?

(Maria goes and helps herself to a bottle of water on the counter.)

Rosa   At church.

Maria   Church. … A lot of good it does him.

Rosa   He goes every Sunday, you know that. Makes an appearance and meets up with all his friends, they talk, maybe have a beer or two afterward.

Maria   *(Looking at her mother working and obviously hot.)* He's out having a beer with his friends and you're here working. Ma, how could you be folding clothes and ironing on a gorgeous sunny day like this?

Rosa   I have to get these done for your father.

Maria   Ma! It's Sunday, a day of rest … and it's nine hundred degrees in here. Do you know they have this great invention … they call it air conditioning. They say it actually cools the air.

Rosa   I have my fan if I get hot.

Maria   *(Picks up the fan.)* This little thing? Ma, really!

Rosa   Your father says it costs too much money to buy an air conditioner.

Maria   I'll buy one for you.

Rosa   *(Lightly with a smile.)* Thanks, but even if you did your father would say the electricity cost too much.

Maria He would at that. He would probably complain that you have no place to store it either. He is so stubborn.

Rosa You know your father and money.

Maria I sure do. *(Picking up a bottle of water.)* I'm surprised he hasn't had a crackdown on bottled water. *(Looking at her mother working and walking over to her.)* Ma, put that down and come to the beach with me.

Rosa Go to the beach? Now?

Maria Yes ... now!

Rosa *(Smiling, realizing that Maria is serious.)* I wish I could, Maria, because it does sound inviting, but I have to get this done and then start to get dinner ready. You know your father likes to eat early on Sunday. *(Looks at the time.)* He should be home soon. He's not going to like that I haven't started it yet.

Maria Ma, it's eleven o'clock in the morning! Most people are not even up yet.

Rosa I was up at seven, made some coffee, and fixed a nice breakfast for your father. He likes his coffee as soon as he gets up.

Maria *(Shaking her head.)* Ma, I don't understand why you are so good to him. What does he do for you?

Rosa He's my husband.

Maria   And you're his wife.

Rosa   He wears the pants.

Maria   And you wear a housedress. Is that fair? … Ma, come with me.

Rosa   Don't be silly.

Maria   Ma, you know I love Daddy, but he's so old-fashioned. It bothers me to see him treat you like this.

Rosa   It's his way.

Maria   But it's not your way is it? … Ma, come on. *(She tries to pry her mother away from her ironing, without success.)* If you don't want to go to the beach, we'll go shopping and have lunch. I know a great place overlooking the ocean. They make some great margaritas there and we could …

Rosa   Margaritas on the ocean? *(She laughs.)* I'm sure it's lovely and I would love to, but like I told you, I have to do this. He'll be home soon. Some other time when your father doesn't need me. *(Beat. Looking at Maria.)* He's not going to like the outfit you have on. Do you have something to put over you in case he comes in?

Maria   No, this is fine! I'm not going to do anything like that. He will just have to realize that this is how I like to dress. I hate that he is still so damn protective of me … like I'm still a little girl.

Rosa   *(Pretending to ignore her daughter.)* Look in my bedroom closet. I think I have a sweater you can throw over that …

Maria NO!

Rosa Then be prepared.

Maria Oh, believe me, I am, after all these years. I could hear him now, *(Mockingly.)* "That's a pretty skimpy dress young lady."

Rosa *(Looking at her somewhat amused.)* Very funny.

Maria Ma, listen to me! *(Grabbing her mother's shoulders to gain her attention.)* Do you know how hard it was for me when I was young, having him constantly checking up on me? I could never do anything. I had to sneak around to do anything. If it wasn't for you, I don't know what I would have done. I could never tell him anything. Even now … to this day, he tells me what I can and cannot do. I hate it.

Rosa He's your father.

Maria He's not my master. Do you remember how when I had a date I had to make up a story about where I was going? I had to pack my clothes in a bag, hide them outside, and then get changed in someone's car. My friends all laughed at me. I was so embarrassed.

Rosa I remember. He was just trying to protect you.

Maria Protect me? He never let me do anything! He never encouraged me do anything beyond clean the house and learn how to cook so I can make a good wife someday. … I remember when I was sixteen, I used to love to draw. I would do it for hours just to express myself. He was fine with that as long as I drew pictures of fruit and trees, but the first time I drew a picture of a woman—a naked woman—he tore it up. He went crazy. Called me names … bad names. He made me feel awful about myself. I stopped drawing. *(Beat.)* And boys … oh my God … they were afraid to come near the house. When I did go out, I had to come home at ten o'clock. Do you know how many times I had to sneak out again?

Rosa   Oh, I know. I was always the one waiting up for you. Do you know how many times I had to tell him you were home so he didn't go searching the neighborhood or have me call your friends?

Maria   Oh, I loved the neighborhood search in the middle of the night. At least you understood me.

Rosa   Maria, you have to remember that where he was born, women are treated differently. He's from the old school. He only had your best interest in mind.

Maria   No! He had his interest in mind. Not mine. If it were up to him I would be a housewife with three kids already. I don't want to be a housewife; I don't want to serve a man all my life. I don't want to serve anyone. I want to be myself, and he stopped me from doing that. I feel that because of him I'll never be able to do what I think I'm capable of doing … doing what I want.

Rosa   Nothing is stopping you. You have your own condo, a good job, good friends, that fancy red car out there, and from what you tell me you can pick and choose the men you want to be with. How much more is there? How bad could it have been? You have done very well for yourself.

Maria   Whatever I did I did it on my own. *(Pointing to her chest each time she says "I.")* Anything that I achieved, I did it in spite of him. I finished school on my own. I got my job on my own. I moved out of crummy town on my own. Everything on my own. Never any support!

Rosa Stop it. That is not true and you know it.

Maria Yes it is, Momma! And yet all the time I have this burning desire to tell him to <u>look at me ... look at what I'm doing. ... Aren't you proud of me</u>? Even now, I always feel I have to get his approval. I'm paranoid to tell him anything ... anything that I like ... anything that I do. I fear his reaction will take the fun out of it.

Rosa He is proud of you.

Maria Well, he could have fooled me.

Rosa He is. He doesn't come out and say it, but I know he's proud of you.

Maria *(Hand gesturing.)* Ah ...

Rosa More than that, he loves you. You cannot deny that. He loves you more than anything. From the day you were born, you were his priority. He did everything he could to try to make you a better life and keep you safe.

Maria Ma, I don't want anyone to make my life anything. I want it to be <u>my</u> life. I'm sick of answering to him and looking for his approval. I just want some support. He has never done anything for me ... ever.

Rosa That's not true.

Maria It is so.

Rosa   Don't let him hear you talk like that.

Maria   Why not? Maybe what he needs is for me to tell him … tell him to let go … to accept me and let me be. *(Looking at her mother working.)* And maybe he needs to hear it from you too. *(Walking over to her mother.)* Look at you. You are an attractive woman. When is the last time you went out dancing or to a show or just for a walk on the beach in the sunset?

Rosa   I'm too old for that.

Maria   You are not. I don't want to hear that. *(Beat.)* Ma, tell the truth. Wouldn't that be really nice? I know you love dancing. I know you like to get dressed up and go out and have fun. Romance?

Rosa   *(Smiling.)* Yes, what woman does not want that? I remember all the places I wanted to go to and all the things I wanted to do. Let me tell you, some of the things I wanted to do would surprise even you. *(Smiles.)* I had dreams just like you do Maria. Believe me, when I was young the furthest thing from my mind was folding men's pants. We did some of those things—romantic things—your father and I, when we first met. He was so handsome back then. He would do anything for me. *(Beat.)* Yes, I do wish your father was more open-minded about those things now, because I still would like to … to walk on the beach in the sunset. *(Laughs.)* It's just something your father won't do.

Maria   Why do you let him get away with that?

Rosa   Get away with what?

Maria   Controlling you like this.

Rosa No one is controlling me. I love him. He gave me my family. Always remember that.

Maria There is more to life than that.

Rosa More than family?

Maria You know what I mean. You have your family. I'm talking about you and doing things that you like.

Rosa Maybe so, but …

Maria But nothing! When Dad comes home, we are going to tell him. We are going to tell him how we feel. We are going to tell him that we have to live our lives too. We are going to tell him that we are sick and tired of him controlling our every move and that he needs to let us breathe.

Rosa I will do no such thing.

Maria Ma, he needs to know.

Rosa Not from me, he doesn't.

Maria Then he is going to hear it from me. I'm going to tell him just how miserable he made my life when I was younger … how I was embarrassed … how he prevented me from doing anything. And I'm going to let him know all that I have done without his support.

Rosa Don't you dare!

Maria No, Momma, the time has come that I have to let him know how I feel. How I have felt all these years.

(The sound of a car door slamming shut can be heard from the outside.)

Rosa   That's him. You better not say anything … and cover up.

Maria   No, I will not, and I have to tell him. The time has come.

Rosa   Maria, I …

(A man in his early 60s enters wearing an old suit jacket and a white shirt and tie.)

Alfredo   Rosa, have you seen my … *(Notices Maria.)* Maria, what are you doing here so early? Dinner is not even ready.

(Instinctively Maria walks over and gives here father a kiss.)

Maria   Hi, Daddy.

Alfredo   *(Looking at Maria's short sundress.)* That's a really skimpy dress, young lady. *(He nods disapprovingly.)* See if your mother has something for you to put on. Then you can help her get dinner ready.

Maria   *(Covering up a bit.)* There is nothing wrong with the dress, and I'm not here to cook. *(Meekly.)* I was headed to the beach.

Alfredo   The beach! You should be headed to church. It's Sunday. Or have you stopped going all together? And I don't want you to go to the beach alone. Men will think you're cheap.

Maria *(To her mother as an aside.)* See what I mean? I can't stand it. Every time!

(Alfredo finds a seat in his favorite chair.)

Alfredo No whispering in my house.

Maria Dad.

Rosa Maria. Don't.

Maria Dad, I want to tell you something.

Rosa Maria!

Alfredo What is it, Maria?

Rosa *(Interrupting.)* What do you want for dinner, Al? I have some chicken in the refrigerator, and I could make some rice.

Alfredo That's fine. How come you haven't started it?

Maria Because it's eleven o'clock in the morn—. … Dad.

Rosa Maria!

Maria Dad, Mom and I were talking about things.

Alfredo Things? What things?

Rosa I'm sure he's not interested, Maria.

Alfredo Woman stuff. I don't care about woman stuff. *(With hand gestures.)* Yak yak yak yak. Talk talk talk.

Maria   That's because you don't listen, listen, listen!

Alfredo   *(Looking at Maria with a smile and nod of the head.)* Just like your mother when she was younger … just like her. … You know, you are starting to look more and more like your mother. You have become a beautiful woman. Time you settled down and started your own family. Beauty does not last forever.

Maria   It does so. You just have to know where to look for it.

Alfredo   *(Realizing the wisdom of Maria's words and turning to Rosa.)* Rosa, we raised a very intelligent girl. *(To Maria.)* You will make a great wife for some young man.

Maria   Dad!

Alfredo   *(Ignoring Maria's question.)* I was telling my friend Carlos about you. He has a son, a lawyer. I was telling him how you finished school and your work. He was impressed; he was going to talk to his son about you. He comes from a good family. It may be nice to meet him.

Maria   Dad, I don't want you setting me up on dates.

Alfredo   He comes from a good family, and that's important. You deserve the best. I want to see that you have it. I won't have it any other way. Not my daughter. Not my little girl.

Maria   I'm not a little girl. You have to stop calling me that.

Alfredo   Nonsense, you will always be my daughter, and I will always have to protect you. That's just how it is when you're a father. You'll understand that someday.

(Maria glances at Rosa, who shakes her head negatively.)

Maria   Dad. I have to tell you something.

Alfredo   What is it that you want to tell me so bad, that it can't wait until after dinner?

Maria   Dad, did you ever stop and think sometimes what you ...

Rosa   *(Interrupting again.)* Maria, can you run to the store for me? I need some bread. Some milk too.

Maria   Not now, Momma.

Rosa   Yes, now, or dinner will be late.

Maria   Ma, will you stop for a minute? I want to tell Daddy something.

Rosa   Maria!

(Maria looks at her mother and sees the concern on her face.)

Maria   Dad. *(Looking directly into his eyes.)* Daddy. *(Holding his hand.)* Dad. *(Looking away back to her mother for consent, which she does not receive.)* Dad. ...

Alfredo   *(Now concerned.)* What is it, sweetheart? Do you need help? Is something bothering you?

Maria   No, I don't need help.

Alfredo I'm always here to help, you know that.

Maria I know, but I'm not looking for help.

Alfredo Then what?

(Momentary silence as they look at each other.)

Maria Daddy … I just want to say. (*Looking at her mother and seeing the concern in her face, and then looking at her father again.*) I just want to say … *(Taking a breath.)* I love you, Daddy.

Alfredo I love you too, Maria. *(They hug warmly.)*

(Looking at Rosa, who is watching close by with a satisfied smile.)

Alfredo I love you too, Rosa.

Rosa And I love both of you.

(Momentary silence as they embrace.)

Rosa Let's go out to lunch … all three of us … right now.

(Alfredo does not like this idea but is given a nudge of encouragement from Maria.)

Alfredo That is a good idea.

Maria I know the perfect spot.

Rosa Let me get ready.

(Rosa packs up a few things quickly and leaves.)

Alfredo   *(Picking up a white shirt from the ironing board as he begins to exit.)* Maria, did I ever tell you how proud I am of you?

(He exits.)

Maria   You just did. Thank you.

End.

Daydreams

Time: The present day, midafternoon in the summer.
Place: The home of Henry and Catherine Dormit.
Setting: The backyard of the house. There is the standard
array of lawn furniture including a lounge chair and table. On
the table are a newspaper and sunglasses.

*(Henry, a middle-aged average family man, enters
dressed in work clothes, carrying a tool box, wearing
work gloves, and looking tired. He lays his tools on
the table.)*

Henry   *(Calling out loud.)* Catherine! ... Catherine, honey.
I think the windows in the back are pretty much done. I just
have the front ones left. ... I'll do them in a bit. I have to pick
up some paint and some brushes. Nice day today. I thought it
was going to rain. ... Catherine!

(No answer.)

Henry   Oh, Catherine.

*(Henry looks around the area, peeks inside windows,
and opens a few doors. He seems to gain energy as he
observes that no one is around.)*

Henry   Catherine, honey! ... I'm ... I'm just going to take
a break for a minute. ... Nice day. *(No answer.)* *(To himself.)*
Good, about time. No one around. *(Deviously.)* I just need
a few minutes. A few minutes alone is all I need. *(He sits
down and looks around.)* Where is the paper? *(Finding the
newspaper and flipping the pages, eventually looking at the*

back page as he relaxes back into the chair.) Yankees are hot. Jeter is a star. Such a young kid. He has everything. Really clutch. They just need one more guy. One more guy and they got it all wrapped up. A new guy, someone that no one ever heard of. *(Drifting off.)*

> *(Flash to the background. A young, tall, handsome man enters dressed in a Yankee uniform and swinging a bat.)*
>
> *(Young autograph seekers gather around, handing the young ballplayer balls, papers, and pens in a frenzy to get his signature. The young ballplayer takes control one at a time.)*

Sports Announcer *(Voiceover, in a big voice)* Hello, New York, this is Jon "Big Gut" Feldman speaking from my gut on NY sports. Just who is this strange visitor to New York, who seems faster than a speeding bullet, more powerful than a locomotive, able to leap tall buildings in a single bound? Well, maybe not. Maybe he's not Clark Kent … but then again, Kent could not hit a curve ball as well as Hank Dormit. Hank Dormit! Get used to the name, folks, where would the Yankees be today had not Hank "The Hulk" Dormit come to town? *(Beat.)* On their way home for the winter, that's where. There is still a mystery surrounding this young and mysterious superstar. *(Suspiciously and softer.)* No one quite knows where he came from or where he's been or what he does in his spare time. *(Changing to a loud tone.)* Quite frankly, no one really cares, as long as the Yankees keep winning. Hank has almost single-handedly turned around New York sports since joining the Yankees in June. He has …

> *(Abruptly from offstage.)*

Catherine   *(Voiceover)* HENRY! ... HENRY!

(Henry wakes up abruptly, almost falling off the lounge chair, and attempts to look busy with his tools.)

(The ballplayer in his daydream disappears while Catherine, a big rather unattractive middle-aged woman, enters with a basket of clothes.)

Catherine   HENR ... oh, there you are. I thought you might have snuck inside to watch the game. Are you done with the windows yet?

Henry   I finished the ones in the back. I just need some spot paint and I'll do those ones in the front.

Catherine   *(Cutting him off.)* So you're not done!

Henry   Almost, I shou—

Catherine   Almost is not done, Henry. Almost gets you nowhere.

Henry   I just need to buy some paint and get some brushes.

Catherine   Well, when are you going to get them? You should have done that yesterday. You know I wanted all this done today. My sister is coming tomorrow, and I won't have my place looking like a barn.

Henry   I know. I thought I had ...

Catherine   It's called planning, Henry. Planning! Knowing what you need before you start something. Knowing not to leave things half-done and half-assed.

Henry   It's just a brush and some compound. I was going to pick it up at Harpell's Lumber in town.

Catherine   In town … you? If you go into town, I won't see you for the rest of the day. McCan's bar doesn't sell brushes, Henry. No, I'm going into town to pick up some things we've been needing for some time. Heaven knows if I wait for you to get up off your swollen behind it will be next year. I'll stop at Harpell's while I'm there. In the meantime, I need you to bring all the summer clothes down from the attic and bring all the winter stuff up. After that, you need to get rid of some of those old suits and clothes that you've had for years, Henry.

Henry   I cleaned out my closet last week. Everything I have I wear.

Catherine   You wear, but they don't fit you anymore.

Henry   They do so.

Catherine   *(Looking at his waistline and laughing to herself.)* Very well, then. At least take them out of the closet and put them in a drawer so I can use the closet space. I have no room for any of my things.

Henry   *(Under his breath.)* Talk about junk.

Catherine   What was that?

Henry   Nothing. I'll make room.

Catherine   I don't like snide comments, Henry. My father always made snide comments to my mother before he died. *(Beat.)* I'll be back in about an hour. Take out something for dinner. God forbid you take me out once in a blue moon.

(She exits.)

(Henry picks up the basket of clothing and starts picking through it.)

Henry   *(To himself.)* Out to dinner? Talk about a pleasant evening and stimulating conversation. *(Looking at the basket of clothes.)* Catherine, where do you want me to put these? In the front or toward the back? … Catherine …

(No answer.)

(Henry stops and looks around to see if the coast is clear. He spots the newspaper again and sits and begins to read an article. Soon he drifts off.)

(A young well-dressed man appears in the background. He is posing for pictures with an Oscar award in his hand. Several young and attractive girls want to be in the picture.)

(Henry is smiling and enjoying his dream. This continues for a while.)

(Catherine enters slowly from behind.)

Catherine   *(Softly into Henry's ear.)* Oh, Henry darling. … Henry, dear, are you having a pleasant dream?

Henry   *(Half-asleep, with a smile on his face.)* Ummm.

Catherine   Ah, relax, dear Henry. … Take your shoes off. … Put your feet up. … Would you like a drink? Let me rub your back. I know those hard muscles of yours must be aching. Relax, dear Henry.

Henry   Ummm. *(She rubs his shoulders and then abruptly squeezes his neck.)* Ahhh!

Catherine   *(Screaming.)* Now get up!

Henry   *(Falls off the chair.)* Cathe … Catherine, you scared me half to death.

Catherine   Really, if I knew I was that close, I would have tried harder.

Henry   That's not a very nice thing to say.

Catherine   Neither is sitting on your ass.

Henry   I just dozed off. I … I don't even remember sitting down. I didn't get much sleep, you know. I haven't had a good night's sleep in some time.

Catherine   *(Shakes her head in disappointment.)* Save it, Henry. I'm leaving; make sure you do as I said so I can relax when I get home. *(She exits, talking to herself.)* I should have listened to Mother. "Don't marry beneath you," she said. She said that.

Henry   *(Mocking her nagging with a hand gesture.)* My day off. I'd rather be working. Anything … washing cars in the car wash, cleaning toilets on the subway, picking up cans from the recycling, garbage. … Must be decent money in that. This is torture. *(Mocking his wife.)* "This is my house, Henry. My house! My father built it with his own hands and hard work … something that you seem to have forgotten. You live here because I let you and because I made the unfortunate mistake of marrying you when I was young and foolish." This is hell!

(Henry picks up the paper again and looks around.)

(A good-looking young man dressed in beach attire enters, surrounded by young girls who are flirting with him.)

(Henry drifts off for a moment, but then wakes up as he drops the paper.)

(Henry sorts the clothes in the basket to take to the attic. The girls disappear but the young man does not. The young man seems to be following Henry around.)

Henry *(To the young man.)* Will you get out of here?

Young Man Me?

Henry Yes, you. Get lost!

Young Man Do you really want that?

Henry Yes, I do!

Young Man No, you don't.

Henry *(Frustrated.)* Can you believe this, even my dreams talk back to me.

Young Man Why do you want me to leave?

Henry Because if you stay in my head, if I allow myself to drift off, I'll never get anything done. I want to have something more to eat tonight besides animal crackers and water.

Young Man   They are better with milk, Henry.

Henry   A comedian.

Young Man   I just read your mind.

Henry   What? Look, I have no time now. Come back tonight when I'm sleeping. Why don't you ever come then?

Young Man   Because then I would be a nightmare. Night dreams are never pleasant. They always feature deceased relatives in a scary situation and are never logical. I leave that to someone else.

Henry   Oh, and this is logical, I suppose?

Young Man   That's not how to look at it.

Henry   It's not?

Young Man   No, daydreams are aspirations, hopes, and pleasantries.

Henry   *(Befuddled.)* They are? Mind if I ask you a question?

Young Man   Go ahead.

Henry   Why do you come here like this? Why do you come to me as a virile young man, with women at his side, a baseball bat in his hand, celebrating a game-winning home run? Or an Academy Award-winning actor? Smart, powerful, creative, wealthy, and handsome. All the things I never was and never will be.

Young Man   You never know.

Henry   A little late for that, wouldn't you say, and even in my best days, I never looked like you. Even in my best days, I never could do what you suggest.

Young Man   That's why it's good to dream, Henry.

Henry   I am well aware of the benefits. Unfortunately, there is also reality.

Young Man   Reality is what you make it.

Henry   Reality is being fifty-five years old and having little to show for it.

Young Man   Dreams can come true, Henry.

Henry   Yeah, yeah, yeah. … Okay, tell you what, we'll swap. You come here, bring up the clothes to the attic, and I'll hit a few home runs and then have an orgy on the front lawn. Wadda ya think?

Young Man   Afraid not, Henry.

Henry   Basket too heavy for you?

Young Man   What makes you think I want to live in your shoes? There's no net gain there. You'd be happy, but I'd be miserable.

Henry   Exactly! So fly away, Mr. Peter Pan. Fly back to

Never Land.

Young Man   Take the next step, Henry. What would happen if you took the next step?

Henry   The next step?

Young Man   The step that frees you. The step you believe is not there, the one you can't see that is impossible to navigate.

Henry   The key word there is "impossible."

Young Man   Nothing is impossible if you think it's possible.

Henry   *(Shaking his head.)* No wonder I missed out.

(Henry looks at the basket of clothing.)

Young Man   Come with me, Henry. Do it now. The time is right.

(The sound of a door being slammed shut and the sound of footsteps are heard offstage.)

Catherine   *(Loudly from offstage.)* Henry!

Young Man   *(More urgently.)* What do you have to lose, Henry? This is not the way it should be. Come with me.

Catherine   HENRY!

Henry   *(Hearing the voice, looking at the basket that has not been moved.)* Where would we go?

Young Man   Pick a spot. You've been to a lot of places, but there are some you might want to explore.

(Henry is silent.)

Young Man   *(Pointing the way.)* Come.

(Henry slowly walks toward the Young Man.)

Young Man   (*Puts his arm around Henry.*) There!

(They begin to walk off.)

Henry   Can we play some golf?

Young Man   *(Takes out a golf ball from his pocket.)* Sounds good. ... Ever make a hole in one?

(They exit.)

Catherine   *(Still offstage.)* Henry, can you get the packages out of the car? ... Henry?

(She enters and notices that the clothing has not been put away.)

Catherine   Henry, it doesn't look like you did anything that I asked. HENRY ... I am talking to you. HENRY!

(She looks around to see if Henry is anywhere near.)

Catherine   *(To herself as see continues to look.)* I married a mouse, not a man. A little tiny itsy bitsy tiny man ... well, I hesitate to use the term man.

(She takes a seat after she is convinced that no one is around.)

Catherine   *(Calling out one last time.)* HENRY. ... Good, finally a chance to relax. *(Noticing a magazine on the table, which she picks up and begins to thumb through.)* This is really lovely; I wish I had that figure. *(She drifts off.)*

(An extraordinarily attractive woman appears in the back walking much like a fashion model. A young man emerges from the other side, kisses her hand, and hands her a rose.)

Announcer   *(Voiceover)* New York society and the paparazzi are abuzz today with the arrival of Catherine De'Louvre from Paris. Catherine's arrival is highly anticipated and will likely be the social event in New York City this year. ...

(A smile appears on Catherine's face.)

(Voice and lights fade.)

End.

A Matter of Choice

Time: Now.

Place: A church.

Setting: Anna, a woman in her 40s, dressed in long dark clothing and a veil, is alone kneeling and praying softly.

Anna   Dear God, I thank you for all you have given me, for making me see the beauty of life, for guiding me and taking care of me, for being with me when I'm alone, for giving me my life and a chance to show you how much I love you. I know you will remember me. I promise with all my heart that I will always be faithful and live my life as only you tell me I should. You are my guide. Give me the strength to follow you and believe in you.

> *(A man and a woman enter from the rear. The man, Frank, is in his late 40s and dressed casually in a sport jacket and open-collared shirt. The woman, Lynn, is early 30s and dressed in a tight short skirt and form-fitting top with high heels and black stockings.)*
>
> *(Anna continues to pray to herself.)*

Lynn   Frank, why are we going into a church? I don't like this. It makes me feel uncomfortable. It gives me the creeps. I haven't been in a church for years. I feel guilty. I feel like I'm going to get struck by lightning. Look how I'm dressed.

Frank   Will you relax? *(Noticing the woman praying.)* I just want to check out something. We won't be long.

Lynn   What is it you want to check out?

Frank   Just a hunch. *(Walking softly and slowly up to the praying woman from behind.)* She's here. I knew it.

Lynn   Who's here?

Frank   See that woman? *(Nodding in Anna's general direction.)* Well, a few years ago, I dated her.

Lynn   *(Talking too loudly.)* What? That old lady in the black dress ... or whatever she has on ... she doesn't look like your type.

Frank   Shush! She's not that old ... about my age ... and, no, she is definitely not my type. Not anymore.

Lynn   Is she a nun?

Frank   No. Although I think she might have done well to become one.

Lynn   *(Tugging at Frank's sleeve.)* Let's not bother her.

(Frank ignores the request and moves closer. He bends over the praying woman.)

Frank   Anna? Anna Tarlini?

(Anna looks up slowly.)

Anna   Yes, that's me. ... Frank? *(Excited.)* Frank!

(She gets up and they hug and kiss on the cheek.)

Frank   I thought it was you, but I wasn't sure until I got close.

Anna   I'm surprised. What are you doing here? Is this your parish? I've never seen you here.

Frank   No, Anna. It's not my parish. I don't really go to church. You know that. But I remember the last time we spoke, you mentioned that you went to church frequently, and I knew you lived in this area.

Anna   That was ten years ago.

Frank   Something like that.

(Anna notices Lynn standing close by.)

Frank   Oh, excuse me. Anna, this is my girlfriend Lynn. Lynn … Anna.

Lynn   Nice to meet you, Anna.

Anna   *(Looking at Lynn almost with contempt.)* Uh huh.

Frank   Do you come here every day?

Anna   Not every day, but whenever I can. Sometimes I'm so busy.

Frank   So how are you?

Anna   Wait, let's move. I don't want to be disrespectful in front of the Lord. Let's go over to the side, away from the altar. We can talk over there.

*(Anna makes the sign of the cross and genuflects.
They move over away from the altar. Lynn stands
close by, notiveably uncomfortable.)*

Frank   So how are you?

Anna   I'm very content right now. He takes care of me.

Frank   By "he" I assume you mean? *(Pointing upward.)*

Anna   Yes, of course. There is no one else.

Frank   I see. ... Do you still travel? Are you doing all the
things you said you wanted to?

Anna   Only if the Lord allows me to. Only if there is a
purpose for me to be elsewhere. There is no reason for me to
see the world when I can see eternity through him.

Frank   *(Surprised.)* I thought you liked to travel ... said
you wanted to go around the world.

Anna   I did once. I don't need to anymore. Besides, I don't
have the time, and I would not enjoy it. It takes me away
from my mission.

Frank   I see. But you know there is nothing wrong with
stopping to smell the roses every now and then.

Anna   Those roses die and eventually crumble into dust. A
momentary illusion of pleasure, as are so many other things
in this world. In his world ... when my moment comes ... I
won't have to stop to smell the roses because the beauty of
those roses will be inside me every moment ... for eternity.

Frank So you really got into this religion stuff.

Anna (*A bit slighted by the remark.*) It's my salvation.

Lynn Frank, we have to be in New York by six.

Frank Wait! We have time.

Lynn There's traffic if we wait too long.

Frank Give me a few minutes.

Anna Don't let me stop you *(Looking at Lynn.)* … from having your fun. *(Beat.)* I see you're still on the prowl.

Lynn On the what?

Frank *(Trying to make light of the comment.)* You're funny … but you know me.

> *(Anna gives Lynn a look. Lynn looks away, embarrassed.)*

Anna Yes, how could I forget?

Frank Ah, we had fun back then. Remember the time we …

Anna I don't think about those times anymore.

Frank Why not?

Anna I have my reasons!

Frank *(Stunned.)* It was a fun time.

Anna   We sinned. I beg the Lord every day to forgive me.

(Anna gives Lynn another contemptuous look.)

Lynn   Frank, this is scaring me.

Anna   *(Accusingly to Lynn.)* Scaring you. Am I scaring you? Well, you should be scared. You should be ashamed. The nerve of you coming into the Lord's house dressed like … like that. Have you no respect?

Lynn   What? Believe me, I didn't plan on coming into a church this afternoon. That was rude. Why did you say that? Just who do you think you are? Who do you …

Anna   I could see the evil inside you.

Lynn   Evil? What do you mean by that? Frank! Listen, I don't know you and you don't know me, but I'll be damned if I let someone talk to me like that.

Anna   You are already damned.

(Lynn takes a deep horrified breath and searches for a response.)

Frank   Easy ladies, this is no place for judgments.

Anna   It is not for me to judge. He is the judge.

Lynn   What nerve.

Frank   Easy, honey. *(Moving Lynn back a bit.)* Anna, calm down. You have no right. *(Pause.)* Why do you say we "sinned"?

Anna Why? Because the Lord told me it was wrong ... the work of the devil. It's the devil who confuses pleasures of the body with my love for Him.

Frank Oh, c'mon, Anna, you can't really believe that. Look around you. Look at the world. Men and women have an attraction. We should enjoy each other. The relationship we had was perfectly natural.

Anna I see you haven't changed. It was immoral! Sex is reserved for creation and creation only. I don't need it, I don't want it, and I regret that I ever did it. I ask him for forgiveness every day.

Lynn Frank. Let's go?

Anna *(Responding to Lynn.)* Why? You don't like hearing about it? Of course not. ... Look at you. The cheapness of how you carry yourself. Parading around in such an evil way. Tempting men to succumb to brief physical pleasures. I could see the devil in you as soon as I laid eyes on you. When is the last time you asked the Lord for help? The Lord can still help you.

Lynn *(Confused.)* I don't feel like the devil's in me. I ... I just feel like ... like a woman.

Anna You do? How do you feel right now? Offering yourself up like an apple for someone to take a bite from. Do you feel compassion, love, caring, the things a woman should feel? No. I bet you just feel those disgusting primal urges. Not love. There is no love in you.

Lynn *(Becoming insecure and defensive.)* I do so have love. Maybe I'm not showing it right now but ... I have love in me. There's a lot of love in me.

Anna   You can't know what love is until he forgives you. Now I only see evil.

Lynn   *(Becoming self conscious.)* Oh, my … Frank, I don't like this. Can I have your jacket? I'm cold. *(Frank takes off his jacket and hands it to Lynn, who puts it on and wraps it tightly around her, covering up as much as possible.)*

Anna   *(Preaching.)* Covering your flesh will not hide what's inside you. Only praying to the Lord will give you strength and contentment. You will feel his love every moment. He will always be there for you … always. You won't have to rely on a coat to hide your cheapness. Get on your knees. Get on your knees now. Ask the Lord to save you.

Lynn   Frank?

Frank   *(Angry.)* Anna, stop it. You really have gone over the edge. You have no right to cast judgment on someone you don't even know just because they dress differently than you. I understand that people need to worship for piece of mind. But you! You never were this mean and intolerant.

Anna   I am a prophet of the Lord.

Frank   I'm sure the Lord is not telling you to be belligerent.

Anna   I carry his word, I am his disciple, I am …

Frank   You're deluded is what you are. And look at you. I don't recognize you like this. I mean, look at you. Is this all you do? Come here and pray? Are you living or have you stopped? Stopped enjoying life. I think you should take off that veil and go out and buy some new clothes and <u>live</u>. For Christ's sake *(Anna cringes.)* let yourself live … enjoy life.

(Beat. Anna looks into Frank's eyes.)

Anna   Who are you to say I'm not?

Frank   Anna!

Anna   *(Calmer.)* I pray for you, Frank. I pray the Lord will take care of you. I know deep down you are a good person. You just need help. The Lord will help you if you let him into your life.

Frank   Stop it. Anna, don't you see what has happened to you? Do you realize how you are living? You're spending your entire life with your head in your hands afraid to pick it up and breathe some life into your lifeless body. *(Anna turns away. Frank follows.)* Do you ever smile? Or do you feel guilty if you do? *(Anna turns away again. Frank follows.)* Do you like to eat? Or would you rather fast? Did you ever think that what you are praying to avoid is exactly what you have become? *(He grabs hold of Anna and turns her so that they are looking into each others eyes.)* Anna, I'm not going to stand here and tell you what to believe and what not to believe in, but I am going to tell you that the life you are living is no life at all.

Anna   You have no right to say that, Frank. You don't know me … not anymore. You don't know what's on my mind. What's in my soul. How I feel. *(Beat. Realizing she went too far.)* Look, I'm sorry, Frank. I got carried away, I'm sorry. I confess that sometimes, I'm a bit intolerant. But I need to show my loyalty to him. I'm not perfect … he understands. I'm sorry if I offended your girlfriend. She is probably very nice.

Frank   She is. She is very nice.

Anna   *(To Lynn.)* I'm sorry; it's just that this is his house.

Lynn   I understand. And I do have love … I'm not an evil person … I'm not a bad person. God knows that … he does, I don't have to tell him, he knows. Frank, I'll meet you outside. This is too much for me. I feel I should go buy a blanket and cover up.

(Lynn exits, pulling her skirt down over her knees.)

Frank   Anna, how did this happen to you?

Anna   How did what happen?

Frank   This … this fanaticism.

Anna   Now who is being judgmental? I don't believe I'm a fanatic. Don't call me that. I know it's hard for you to understand, but I really am quite happy. I know I live my life differently than others, but that's my choice. It's my choice, Frank, and I will not change it. *(Beat.)* I'm sorry I scared your girlfriend. I'm usually not that way. I just was not expecting to see you … see you come in dressed like a playboy with a girl twenty years younger than you on your arm. I just wasn't expecting it. I'm human too, you know. I have feelings. Were you trying to embarrass me?

Frank   Heavens, no. Why would you think that?

Anna   Then why did you come in? Why? To show yourself off to this wretched old woman praying like a fool to a God that you don't understand nor believe in? To show your lady friend how foolish a woman can become? To laugh about me at your next cocktail party?

Frank   No. Of course not. I just …

Anna   Then why? *(Momentary silence.)* Yes, I know I'm different. I see what goes on around me, but my life is my choice. <u>My choice.</u> It's how I want to live. It gives me fulfillment the only way I know how to find it. I believe in what I believe in. This is not entertainment; I'm not a performer. I neither expect people to understand it nor follow in it. Just leave me to be myself in my own way. The alternative is just not for me, and I tried the alternative, as you well know.

Frank   I understand, Anna. I do, and it sure was not my intention to embarrass you or in any way suggest you change from what makes you happy. *(Beat. Changing the subject.)* My, ten years without seeing you, and we almost get into an argument. I didn't want that.

Anna   Neither did I.

Frank   I just had a hunch that you may be here, and since I was in the area I took a shot. I wanted to see you, say hello. And it is good to see you, I mean that.

Anna   Thanks. It's good to see you too. You still are an attractive man. *(She smiles.)*

Frank   *(Noticing the smile.)* There you go. That wasn't that hard, was it?

Anna   *(Smiles broadly.)* No.

(Frank lightly runs his hand across her smile.)

Frank   You're pretty when you smile.

Anna   *(Looking down, a bit embarrassed.)* Thank you.

Frank   Anna. I think about you ever so often.

Anna   I have flashbacks myself.

Frank   We went out every Friday night … all the great restaurants … all the shows. It was fun back then … at least for me.

Anna   *(Momentary reflection.)* Back then, maybe. Maybe, back then, there were some good moments. *(No longer reflective, returning to current life.)* But people change, Frank. As time goes on, we are better able to put the past into perspective and understand it, now that we are older and wiser. We learn from our mistakes.

Frank   Mistakes? *(Looks directly at Anna, shakes his head, and sighs deeply.)* Look, I have to leave. Lynn is probably outside stamping her feet … waiting.

(Frank starts to turn to leave.)

Anna   So long, Frank. I'll pray for you.

(Frank stops.)

Frank   Anna, would you mind if I ask you one personal question? I just have to know.

Anna   Nothing too personal, I hope?

Frank   No, of course not.

Anna   Go ahead.

Frank   Well, people don't … don't usually turn so fervently to religion unless something happens to them. They have a vision or a near-death experience, or something traumatic happens to them.

Anna   Not necessarily.

Frank   More often than not.

Anna   I guess.

Frank   Anna, why? What happened? Something happened. Tell me?

Anna   *(Reluctantly, after looking at Frank.)* Yes, you are right. Something did happen that changed me. Something that I had a hard time coping with until the Lord came down to me and explained it. It was hard for me to give all I had, all the love and caring I thought I possessed, and not have it returned. To give all I have and feel worse after having expended the effort. The Lord showed me how weak I was, that my love was misplaced, and that following him and giving my life to him will have its reward. A reward far more powerful than anything this earth or my body can give.

Frank   What was it? Please tell me.

Anna   You don't have any idea, do you?

Frank   No.

Anna   It was you, Frank. It was you!

End.

The Hired Hand

Time: Current day around 10:30 AM.
Place: The New York City apartment of Linda Vickers.
Setting: Linda, an attractive woman in her mid-30s, is
dressed in business attire and sitting at her kitchen table
fumbling with papers and talking on the phone. The kitchen
is messy, with various pots, pans, and dishes scattered about.

Scene One

Linda   *(On the phone.)* Hello. Is this Manhattan Electrical? ...
I'm Linda Vickers. I called last week for a lighting installation.
Your man was supposed to be here between eight and ten today.
It's now ten thirty. Eleven thirty? No, that is not good. I arranged
my schedule specifically to be here at ten o'clock. I expected
that you would have someone here at that designated time. ...
I really don't care that you're busy. So am I. ... Well, if you
can't accommodate me, then you may as well call your man
up and tell him to turn the truck around and go back because I
will not be here. ... No, next week is not acceptable. ... Don't
be sorry, be on time.

   (Hangs up.)

Linda   Damn it!

   *(Julie, Linda's friend and neighbor, enters all
   excited carrying a newspaper. Julie is an average-
   looking woman in her mid-30s, dressed casually in
   sweatpants and a sweatshirt.)*

Julie   Tell me this is not you.

Linda What's not me?

Julie This ad.

Linda What about it?

Julie What about it? *(Reading from the paper.)* "Wanted: one male 30–40. Must be reliable, organized, and able to perform all household chores from plumbing to dishwashing. *(Looking up and then back to the paper.)* Performance of intimate husbandly duties will also be required from time to time on an as-needed basis. Long-term relationship are neither required nor desired, but applicant must be mature, attractive, and well-endowed. Some long hours should be expected, but pay is excellent. If interested, call Linda." … Then it gives your number. That's how I knew it was you.

Linda So?

Julie So? Are you crazy? Do you know what kind of nuts you're going to attract with this type of ad? Don't you know how this sounds? It sounds like you want to have a man come over here and do … do everything!

Linda I do.

Julie You do?

Linda Yes, I do. *(Julie gives Linda a look.)* I know how it sounds, and I know I have to be careful, but the more I thought about it, the more I became convinced that is what I need.

Julie Need what?

Linda   To rent a husband.

Julie   Linda, you have gone over the edge. For a woman as successful as you and with your intelligence, you have gone right over the edge.

Linda   I don't think so.

Julie   Well, I do. Look, you just got divorced six months ago, and I understand that you may be feeling a bit uncertain about what is going to happen, but you are still an attractive woman. I'm sure you will find the right man soon. Just give yourself some time.

Linda   Julie, you just don't understand. First of all, this divorce thing is no big thing ... not anymore. I've been through it three times now. Three times! What that tells me is that marriage is not for me. Some women need it, but I sure don't. I have my own career to take care of. I make more in one month than most men make in a year. I certainly don't need anyone for financial support, and I'm certainly not going to stroke any under-achieving male's ego when they realize that.

Julie   So you need to find a rich man.

Linda   No, I don't. We'd be competing with each other all the time. He'd be telling me just how great a job he's doing or how much money he has or how smart he is. Always trying to one-up me. I won't have that.

Julie   So then what's the point?

Linda   What point?

Julie Of this ad. What possessed you to place an ad like this in the paper?

Linda Because its readers are generally those who are the most educated and ...

Julie That's not what I mean.

Linda Because I need someone I can count on to do things around the house.

Julie A maid?

Linda No, not a maid. I need a man. Someone who can fix leaks, mow the lawn, move furniture, shovel snow ... you know what I mean.

Julie Fixing leaks, mowing the lawn, and all that is fine, I understand. But what about "intimate husbandly duties" and "must be well-endowed"?

Linda Well.

Julie Well what?

Linda I want that too.

Julie Want what ... sex?

Linda Yes, of course. I'm human. I have physical needs like everyone else. Just because I'm single doesn't mean I've lost my libido.

Julie I'm sure you will have plenty of opportunities. All you have to do is get out of the house every once in a while.

There are other things in life besides your job, you know. Go out and see what's out there.

Linda That's just it. I don't want go out on the prowl. I don't want to be flirting around the bars hoping some guy will buy me a drink, pick me up, and screw me in his hotel room. I don't like that. Such bullshit. I have to listen to, "Oh, I love your hair. Oh, you are so funny, your eyes are so lovely, you're a deep person, so interesting." My God, I can't stand it.

Julie I know what you mean. Believe me, I do. I have to do it myself sometimes, and there are times when I feel like I'm on sale, but how else do you meet a man and have a meaningful relationship?

Linda So you know why I put that ad in the paper.

Julie I do?

Linda Yes, except that I'm not looking for a relationship.

Julie You're not?

Linda No. Just someone to do things that I need done and to have sex with every now and then.

Julie Sex every now and then?

Linda Yes. Is that so bizarre? If I want sex, I don't want to have to go out and search the city streets for someone who measures up. I want to have someone around where I can say, let's have at it *(Snaps her fingers.)* and he obeys.

Julie A husband for hire?

Linda   Exactly!

Julie   Maybe you should call him "the contractual cock."
(*Laughing.*) You've lost it. What about a relationship?

Linda   No. Not for me. Like I told you, like I said in the ad,
I am not looking for any relationship. Just someone to do the
things around the house that I can't get to nor want to get to,
and someone to have sex with when and if I want.

Julie   Linda, I'm not an expert or anything, but I don't
know about this. First of all, you are going to get all
sorts of loonies coming to your door—and there goes the
neighborhood—and secondly *(Emphasizing.)* why do you
want sex without a relationship? It never is any good for me.
I really don't enjoy it when it's that way.

Linda   Well, I do. For me, sex is just physical. Get it hard,
stroke it, suck it, stick it in, and pound away. Then I can go
back to work.

Julie   Then back to work? Sounds like your priorities are a
little mixed up, don't you think?

Linda   No, I've thought about it for a long time, and I am a
good judge of people, especially men.

Julie   Is that so? How many times have you been divorced?

Linda   Really funny. Let's just say I'm wiser from the
experience.

Julie   I'd love to see the cast of candidates that you get on
this one. What do they put on their resume?

Linda   Well, stick around because my first interview should be here soon. *(Looking at the time.)* As a matter of fact, real soon. If he's one minute late, I'll tell him to go home.

Julie   Well, you know he may have to clear it with his parole officer. What if he is married?

Linda   Married? *(Beat.)* I hadn't thought of that. No, that probably won't work. Not enough to go around. But then, if he performs, maybe it has some ...

> *(The doorbell rings.)*

Linda   *(Looking at her watch.)* Good, right on time.

Julie   Want me to leave?

Linda   No, stick around, you may learn something.

> *(Linda goes to the door and opens it. A tall extremely good-looking man enters. He is muscular with a slim waist, dressed tastefully in a polo shirt and neatly pressed slacks.)*

Peter   Hello, I'm looking for Miss Linda Vickers.

Linda   That's me. You must be Peter. *(She extends her hand.)*

Julie   *(Admiring the merchandise.)* Appropriate name.

Linda   Nice to meet you, Peter. This is my neighbor, Julie.

Peter   Nice to meet you, Julie.

Julie   Likewise.

Linda   Come in so we can get started. *(Pointing to the table.)* Have a seat. *(They sit.)*
Coffee, water?

Peter   No, thank you.

Linda   Peter, Julie is going to sit in with us. We are close friends and this job is a bit—well, unique—so I want her to be comfortable with you.

Peter   That's perfectly fine.

Linda   Peter, I don't want to beat around the bush. I'm a very busy and demanding woman. I need someone who can do everything around the house that I can't get to. Everything—throw out the garbage, do laundry, make coffee, install lights, put up decorations, rearrange furniture, make my appointments—the works. What's your experience?

Peter   Well, for the past five years I've been the domestic affairs controller for a Barry Mandris.

Julie   The singer?

Peter   Yes. I took care of everything in his domestic estate. Everything from making coffee and installing an intercom system to waking him up in the morning and cleaning up after his dog. I have a degree in mechanical engineering from Columbia and worked as an auto mechanic prior to that. I am fully confident I can do everything you need done.

Julie   Is Barry gay?

Peter I don't get involved in personal issues.

Linda Perfect. You did say … everything.

Peter Yes. I believe so. From what you have mentioned so far I have no prob—

Linda You read the ad?

Peter Yes, of course.

Linda Any questions?

Peter I think it was pretty clear.

Linda It was? Tell me just to make sure.

Peter I'll be glad to. In addition to what you just mentioned, you want someone to, and excuse me if I'm blunt, but just to be perfectly clear, you want someone to fuck when you want to. Is that right?

Julie That's hitting the nail on the head.

Linda Yes.

Peter And you do not want to have any personal relationship with this person.

Linda Exactly.

Peter And I can show you that I would meet the endowment requirement.

(He stands up and begins to unbuckle his pants.)

Linda   That won't be necessary.

Julie   Oh, Linda, that's the fun part.

Linda   Julie, behave.

Julie   Peter, are you married? If you don't mind my asking.

Peter   Divorced … twice.

Linda   That's good. I've been down that road myself, and that's about all I will tell you about my personal life. I am very serious about not wanting any intimate relationship that we may have to build into anything beyond the physical act. Is that clear?

Peter   Yes, that is clear.

Linda   I don't want questions about what I do, where I've been, who my friends are, or who my family is. That type of talk is not appropriate for this assignment. Is that clear?

Peter   Yes, ma'am.

Linda   Further, I don't want to know anything about your personal life. Nothing! All I expect is that you do your job exactly as I prescribe and be ready when I call for those other services. That may involve working some off hours, but it usually would not be too long. Although I hope you're not a minute man.

Julie   He looks like he can go on for hours.

Linda   Julie! You'll have to pardon my friend, this is new to her.

Peter No problem.

Linda You'll have your specified days off, and I'll try not to bother you at inappropriate hours. Any questions?

Peter Salary?

Linda Yes, of course. *(She writes a number down on a piece of paper and hands it to Peter.)* Is that good to start with?

Peter Yes, it's fine.

Linda I will review your performance in six months, and if everything is to my liking I'll see if I can do a little better. Do we have a deal?

Peter We do.

Linda Good, be here Monday at six AM sharp. I like a full breakfast.

(She shows him to the door.)

End Scene One.

Scene Two

Time: Six months later.
Place: Linda's kitchen.
Setting: Linda is seated alone sipping coffee. The kitchen is noticeably well kept-up and there is less clutter around the table.

(A knock on the door.)

Linda   Come in, it's open.

(Julie enters.)

Linda   Well, greetings, stranger. Where have you been?

Julie   Good morning, I've been sort of busy lately. I saw your car outside, how come you're home?

Linda   Just felt like taking a day off.

Julie   That's not like you.

Linda   I know, but I've been able to catch up on virtually everything since Peter's been on board. Look around, I bet you hardly recognize the place. Everything is in order, everything works.

Julie   That's nice.

Linda   He is really a godsend. There is nothing he can't do.

Julie   You're happy with him, I take it.

Linda   Oh, yes. In every way. *(Smiling.)* If you know what I mean. He is a bit quiet, though. Today is his six-month review, and I decided that I'm going to allow him to open up more.

Julie   I thought that is what you did not want to happen? No relationship, remember?

Linda   Yes. I know. But lately I've been thinking that I may be able to relax that condition a little. I mean, I think I know him well, but I want to get to know a little more about him. I want to tell him more about me. In the few conversations we did have, he seems so caring … intelligent. He is really a lovely man. *(Beat.)* I hate to admit it, but I think you were right some months ago, sex and relationships do go hand in hand.

Julie   I see. How do you think he is going to feel about that?

Linda   Oh, I'm sure he'll be fine with it. I could tell he wants to open up with someone. Me, who else does he have? I don't think he has anyone that he's really close with. Poor man.

Julie   How would you know that?

Linda   Just my feminine instincts.

(The doorbell rings.)

Linda   That must be him. Julie, if you don't mind, I will need to talk to Peter privately about his review. So if you don't mind, just hello and have a nice day, and then scram.

Julie   Oh, of course.

(Peter enters.)

Peter   Good morning, Miss Vickers.

Linda   It's Linda. Peter, you remember Julie, don't you?

Peter   Ah. … Yes, of course. Good morning, Julie.

Julie   Good morning.

Linda   Julie was about to leave so we can begin with your review.

Julie Okay, take care.

(She begins to leave but Peter stops her.)

Peter No, wait. Stay.

Linda Peter, this is a private matter.

Peter No, it's not. Not anymore. This entire charade has got to stop.

Linda That is exactly what I had wanted to talk to you about. It's time we opened up a bit. I know that has been on your mind, and I'm willing to work with you on it.

Peter Miss Vickers, you are blind.

Linda What?

Peter Miss Vickers, for the past six months I've come here virtually every day doing everything your little heart desired. We never talked about anything meaningful. Most of the time I was here all day by myself.

Linda Don't worry. I can fix that.

Peter All by myself. *(Beat.)* Except for Julie. *(He takes hold of her hand.)* If it wasn't for her, Miss Vickers, I don't think I could have lasted this long. Julie would come over and we'd have coffee and chat about anything. I needed that, Miss Vickers. It was so terribly lonely here day after day. She's a lovely woman.

(Linda is horrified.)

Julie   I wanted to tell you, Linda.

Linda   Skip it.

Peter   I hope you understand, Miss Vickers. This job has got to end. Now. If I'm going to play husband, I might as well do it for real. *(Holding Julie tight.)* Julie and I got married yesterday.

Linda   Julie, how could you do this to me?

Julie   I'm sorry, Linda. It just sort of happened. I didn't think he meant anything to you.

Linda   You should have asked.

Julie   You would not have admitted it, would you?

Linda   I suppose not.

(They begin to leave.)

Julie   Wish me luck, Linda.

Linda   Go!

(They exit.)

(Linda moves slowly to the table and pulls out a piece of paper and a pen.)

Linda   *(To herself.)* Wanted. One male 30–40 must be personable and reliable and open for a long-term....

End.

Diplomacy

Time: The year 2019. Mid-February.
Place: The office of the president of the United States, Linda Gerard.
Setting: The president is seated alone in her office looking over some documents on her desk. She is dressed in formal business attire and looks tired and concerned. On her desk there is a phone, stacks of paper, and various pictures of family and times gone by. Behind her desk, hanging in full center view, is the American flag. The faint sounds of crowd noise can be heard from outside. At times, angry voices in the crowd become clear as they shout out profanities.

(Linda gets up to look out the window. The buzzer rings on her intercom. Linda turns to answer.)

Linda   Yes, Carol.

Carol *(Voiceover from the intercom.)* Linda, the secretary of state and General Abrams are here.

Linda   Send them right in, Carol, and no interruptions for the next hour or so.

(She picks up a picture and looks at it for a moment. The general (Carl) and the secretary of state (Don) enter.)

Carl   Good morning, Madam President.

Don   Good morning.

Linda   Good morning, gentlemen.

Carl   You look fine this morning.

Linda   Knock it off, Carl. Now is not the time for patronizing. *(With a hand gesture.)* Have a seat.

(Don sits. Carl stands in military at-ease.)

Linda   Any problems getting in?

Carl   No.

Don   There was a small crowd out by the front gate, but that is to be expected.

Linda   It is?

Carl   *(Instantly reaching for his phone.)* I'll have security take care of it.

Linda   Later. I don't want to provoke anything.

Carl   A simple phone call and …

Linda   Later! Let's get to business. I called you in here because we are on the verge of a national calamity that we need to do something about today.

Carl   Yes, we do.

Don   I agree, the situation is rather serious.

Linda   Don, have you been in touch with the Canadians?

Don *(Somewhat evasive.)* Yes, I talked with the Prime Minister about an hour ago.

Linda And?

Don He says he will do what he can but can't promise us anything.

Linda Did you mention our urgency?

Don Yes, I did, and I was diplomatically blunt so that he fully understood the situation.

Linda That's good. Go on.

Don He expressed his concern and promises to do what he can, but he could not offer us anything concrete in the short term.

Linda Short term being what?

Don Three months … maybe six.

Linda That is unacceptable.

Carl Six months! You said he understood?

Don I don't like it either. He said they are increasing production as much as possible, but they will need every drop of crude that they can squeeze out of those oil sands to meet their own needs.

Carl Nonsense. They have plenty to spare.

Don He said that the winter has been exceptionally rough and …

Carl *(Interrupting, annoyed.)* Winter, winter, winter. It's winter everywhere.

Don *(Continuing his assessment.)* Consumption is unusually high, and production has virtually stopped in the Northern Territories. Some facilities won't be back up until May … so … June, July at best.

Carl We should insist!

Don And just what good would that do, Carl? We are not going to start a war with Canada.

Carl Our national economy is at stake! We cannot at this point sit down and become victims!

Linda Calm down, Carl. Let's understand the entire situation before we jump to conclusions and make a mistake. What is the situation in the Middle East?

Don We are opening some doors diplomatically and …

Carl The situation is grim. The Chinese have control of virtually all of the oil coming out of the entire area. The Saudis are done. King Fassad yielded the palace and promised cooperation with Beijing. The fields in Iraq and Iran have been commandeered by Chinese Nations. All production is being controlled by them. What little shipments are getting out are going to the Far East.

Linda What about President Amid?

Carl *(Sarcastic laugh.)* Nowhere to be found. He could be dead.

Linda What about our Kurdish friends and the all the oil ministers and executives that we supported?

Carl What about them?

Linda I'm sure they know how to obtain a supply, even if it's temporary.

Carl Madam President, those people threw up their hands as soon as the situation turned south and the Chinese entered. They cut a deal for themselves and got the hell out of there.

Linda You agree, Don?

Don Unfortunately, yes. I am so very disappointed in their reaction. I considered those people our friends, with good values and high principles, and that they appreciated ...

Carl *(Cutting in.)* We have no friends, Don, and there aren't any principles. Not now.

Linda That's not true. How about Europe?

Don Totally reliant on Russia.

Carl Who, I may add, is using the opportunity to do all the things we would have gone to war over in the sixties.

Don All of Europe is so scared to upset the Russians they won't even talk to us.

Carl See what I mean about friends?

Linda What about the South? Brazil, Venezuela, even Argentina?

Carl   Forget the last two. Brazil has plenty of fuel, but it is not compatible with our machines.

Don   We have several retooling operations in progress, and our research with ethanol, lithium-based energy cells, and solar power is coming along quite nicely.

Carl   We are years away.

Don   Not years.

Carl   Yes, years! And since most of that research is done abroad we stand a chance of losing it to some military coup or religious jihad.

Linda   *(Getting up from her desk, reacting to both the conversation and the crowd noise.)* How could this happen so fast?

Carl   How could this happen so fast? Well, I'll tell you! Two billion people, that's how. Every able-bodied Chinese man, woman, and child in the action. Sheer numbers, that's how. Overwhelming numbers. It's a matter of survival to them. Their economy is three times as large as ours and just sucks up every drop that is produced.

Linda   And we helped build it.

Carl   That we did. That we did indeed. We educated their people, invested in their infrastructure, opened our borders, and shared our technology. We exported our jobs and manufacturing plants, and let them ship any piece of crap they made in here at a fraction of what we can produce it for.

Linda   That's free trade, Carl. You were a supporter.

Carl   It's not free when labor is less than one dollar an hour.

Linda   Don, any hope of reaching a diplomatic compromise with Beijing or working a deal with the locals in Hong Kong?

Don   Diplomacy is always an option.

Carl   Diplomacy is an option if you have something they want. We have nothing! They are a solid core bound by their genes.

Linda   There are millions of Chinese who live here in the U.S.

Carl   Not as many as there were five years ago, or two years ago for that matter. They migrated back after we gave them free education and money to spend.

Linda   That's unfair, Carl. You are not being helpful. What about the Saudi resistance? The Muslim coalition?

Carl   Oh, come on. All of us know, or should have known, Don, that they would be ineffective. Those people were unable to put down a street riot. They were ill-trained; ill-equipped, not motivated, and have no guts.

Linda   How do you explain that, Carl? Our own army took over the training and recruitment years ago. When we turned it over, I was told they were ready for anything.

Don   I was told the same thing, General.

Carl   You were told wrong! The people you put in charge of intelligence just told you what you wanted to hear, overestimated their ability and desire. What's more, they never fully understood how "those people" think. Now, they consider that we abandoned them. Left the area in ruins economically, politically, and morally.

Linda   That is not true. We gave them our full support. Encouraged self-rule and tolerance. We sunk a lot of money into their economy and those oil fields based on our belief in that policy. What more could we do?

Carl   *(Loudly.)* We could have looked out for ourselves, that's what we could have done!

Don   Easy, General.

Carl   I'm sorry, but with all due respect, Madam President and Mr. Secretary … we fucked up. We let the entire region— the region on which our entire economy depends—slip away. Ten years ago, we had the opportunity to protect our interests. Do whatever we needed to. Take control of whatever we needed … all of it. But no, we had no right to take what is not ours. We had no right to consider our own needs. Well, Madam, the country will now have to pay the price for years of liberal diplomacy and, as you called it, tolerance.

Linda   It was the right thing to do, General. I was elected on that principle, and I intend to abide by my principles.

Don   *(Forcefully.)* Now is not the time for principles, Madam. This is a time for war. If you studied your history, you would have realized that in times of need, you have to take. Consequences will be erased over time.

Linda   *(Angrily.)* I won't hear any more of that.

(Crowd noise intensifies from outside, now mixed with screams.)

Carl Would you rather hear that?

(Carl gets up and walks toward the back.)

Linda Don, what is our internal supply situation?

Don Alaska is pumping what they can, but since the environmental shutdown two years ago maintenance is an issue. The flow has not been reliable, maybe 20 percent of normal. Some of it is getting into Seattle, but distribution after that has been problematic, and prices are extreme.

Carl I hear that up there, if you can't get it, you steal it. Oil piracy has come of age. Tankers are being hijacked, and drivers are armed. We are returning to the Middle Ages.

Linda I'm sure that's an exaggeration, General. Stick to the facts. What about the Gulf?

Don The Gulf is paralyzed. What little production there is is being held at the ports because we have no way to transport it any further.

Linda Have we mobilized the National Guard?

Don We have, but many have not shown up.

Linda Well, that I cannot tolerate. This is a national emergency. It is their job and responsibility! Send word that anyone not reporting for duty will be arrested.

Don They can't find transportation, Linda. They have no fuel.

Linda What do you mean, they have no fuel?

Carl   It means they will have to walk.

Linda   Can we pick them up in a convoy?

Don   We should be able to arrange that. General Abrams, what do you think?

Carl   Logistically difficult, and it will take at least a week … best case.

Linda   Get it done, General.

Carl   If that is what you want to do, Madam, then that is what we will do.

Linda   It's not what I want to do, General, it is what we have to do. I just can't believe that I had to come up with that idea and this situation has not been rectified. Where are our emergency plans?

(Crowd noise is now loud.)

Carl   What plans are those, Madam? You mean the ones that were cut out of the budget and sent off to foreign aid?

Linda   Cut it out, General. Just get it done.

Carl   I'll call General Norton in New Orleans.

(He walks off.)

Don   Madam, you should be aware that in the Northeast people are fighting over the small amounts available. Many have fled the area and are heading south. The roads are choked with cars, complicated by breakdowns along the way.

People are cold, hungry, and frustrated. Some are on foot and headed to Washington looking for answers … answers that we may not have. Linda, I'm concerned for your safety and others here in Washington.

Linda   I'm doing the best I can, Don.

Don   I know you are, Linda, but the crowds are becoming angry mobs.

Linda   *(Hearing the crowd noise and reacting to it.)* Don't they understand that this also affects me, my family, and my children?

Don   I'm sure they do.

Linda   Then why, Don? Why? I always did what was right, what was fair.

(Don does not answer, as both hear the crowd noise and realize the potential threat.)

Linda   Anything we can do to contain the flow?

Don   We may try to put up blockades on the major roads and have the streets of the Capital patrolled by our armed forces.

Linda   That's extreme, don't you think?

Don   Madam, judging from the noise I'm hearing from out front, we may have no choice.

(Carl reenters.)

Carl   Madam, I just spoke to our Commander down in New Orleans. He said that because of resource limitations it would be next to impossible to round up, by convoy, all our troops. He suggested that we enlist local civilians to help out.

Linda   I don't think we could find that many volunteers in such short a timeframe.

Carl   They won't be volunteers, Linda.

Carol   *(Voiceover from the office intercom.)* Linda, I have just been advised by gate security that protesters are entering the White House grounds.

Don   Madam. I'm concerned. You should evacuate.

(Don tries to escort Linda to the door.)

Linda   *(Resisting.)* No! I have to talk to them. Send notice that I will talk to them on the front lawn in ten minutes.

Carl   You risk assassination.

Linda   I know what I have to say. We need calm, unity, faith. We can survive this. I know that. We have for over two hundred years. They will understand.

Carl   You may not get that chance. They are not in an understanding mood.

Linda   I'll have to try. *(Presses the intercom.)*

Don   Linda, I don't think …

Linda   Carol, please inform security that I will be delivering a live message for the American people on the front lawn at noon and to remain calm and in control. *(Beat. Pressing the button again.)* Tell them that I don't want anyone hurt and that we can get over this.

(No answer.)

Linda   Carol ... *(Pounding the button.)* Carol ... Carol!

(Crowd noise intensifies.)

Don   Madam, the helicopter is on the roof. I'll call.

(He walks to the side and dials his cell phone.)

(Carl instinctively tries to show Linda the way out.)

Linda   *(Again resisting.)* Wait, where are we going?

Carl   That's top security. We have choices, we will review on-board.

Linda   What about Amanda and Christina?

Carl   Don't know.

Linda   Don't know! Well, I have to know that my children are protected.

Carl   I'm sure they will be fine.

Linda   How do you know that?

(Crowd noise closer, words can now be understood.)

Carl I don't, but I do know we have to go. *(He guides her toward the exit.)* Don, is that helicopter ready? ... Don?

(Don motions with his hand for them to stop as he continues to listen to a voice on the other end of the cell phone. After a moment, he addresses them.)

Don We have a problem. ... No gas!

(Crowd noise gets loud. Fade to black.)

End.

The Best of Friends

Time: Now.

Place: Anywhere.

Setting: A living room. Two men (Richard and Dick) enter walking in synchronized steps and close together. Both are between 35 and 45 years of age. Richard walks confidently and straight up, while Dick (the smaller of the two) walks close behind, hunched over and seeming uncomfortable. They sit down on two chairs facing each other. Richard sits up straight while Dick sits extremely slumped over with his head down and hands hanging over the sides of his chair.

Richard *(With a deep sigh.)* Wow, that was a long day. It just dragged on and on. I am glad it's over. *(He adjusts his pants at the crotch and loosens his belt.)*

Dick *(Sits up a bit.)* Thanks! I need to breathe. Thank God it's Friday.

Richard Tell me about it.

Dick No, you tell me. What's on the agenda?

Richard I don't know just yet. I just got in. I'm sort of tired right now. *(Leans back on the couch to relax.)*

Dick Oh, no! Not again! Not this weekend! I can't stand being cooped up like this. I need to get out too, you know. You're not the only one who needs to work out to stay in shape.

Richard Will you relax? We'll do something.

Dick I don't want to relax. I relax all day. Try to let you do your thing. Stay out of your head. But now it's my time. *(Beat.)* It's almost six, and you haven't made any plans.

Richard All right, all right, what a pest. … Maybe I'll call Annie.

Dick *(Raising up a bit from his slouched position.)* Annie! Oh, I like her! Last time she wore that blue denim, really short-short miniskirt. *(Raising up a bit more.)* She has a great butt. I was eying it all night. Yeah, call her.

Richard She sure is a good-looking girl. Gorgeous hair and face. *(Laughs a bit.)* Maybe a bit too young for me. I don't think she's over thirty, and she is sure not the brightest light.

Dick *(Raising up more.)* Why do you give a shit? You're not asking her to add and subtract. All that matters is that she's hot. That's it! Shit, we came so close last time. You had her alone, on your couch with her bra off and moaning with passion, but you didn't pull the trigger. Damn, that was painful for me. My head was throbbing. I felt like a tiger in a cage that was shrinking, and I couldn't get out.

Richard Will you relax, we were just making out. Besides, that was our first real date. I wanted to find out a little more about her. I didn't want her to think I had only one thing on my mind.

Dick What? What else is there? How many times have I told you about this relationship crap? That comes later. You have to get laid first or the other part will be no good, no how.

Richard You have a one-track mind.

Dick Damn right, I do! *(Beat.)* Well, not quite.

Richard Yes, I forget about that.

Dick *(Proudly.)* Well, don't, and while we're on the subject, try not to drink too much. It gets in the way of more important things.

Richard I have to have something to loosen me up.

Dick Smoke some dope or something. You know how I get when you drink too much. Stop the BS and call Annie.

Richard *(To himself as Dick gets more and more fidgety.)* Annie. Yes. Let me look up her number. *(Finding it on the cell phone directory.)* Here it is. *(Begins to dial.)* Wait, if I remember right, Annie likes to go out for French food and have wine with dinner. Expensive wine no less. The last bottle cost me three hundred bucks. Damn! What are we going to talk about? I don't know if I want to listen to stories about her friends back in college or life in Buffalo or wherever she's from. *(Shaking his head negatively.)* We have absolutely nothing in common. She didn't even know that the Red Sox came from Boston. Can you imagine that? Last time at dinner we had to observe several moments of silence until I thought of something to say. No, I don't think this is a good idea. *(Starts to put away the cell phone.)*

Dick No! Pick up that phone! You think too much. Let me think for you.

Richard You get me in trouble when you think.

Dick So what? You have to take a shot every now and then, or what would life be like? C'mon, think of that skirt ... her

133

legs … her butt. *(Starts to get excited again.)*

Richard Umm, her butt did look divine in that skirt. Umm. I think she was wearing a thong …

Dick *(Now almost up straight.)* Yes. Now you're talking. Can you imagine what would be underneath that skirt? Think of that first touch … the first whisper of passion … peeling off her clothes. Call her! Now! Tell her to wear something erotic. Maybe black stockings … high heels …

Richard Stop it! I'm not telling any woman what to wear. *(Beat.)* I don't know if I have the money to go out tonight.

Dick Forget the money, think of it as an investment, and believe me payback time will be worth it.

Richard She is pretty sexy. Okay, you win. *(Begins to dial.)*

(The phone rings.)

(A beautiful young sexy woman enters from the right dressed only in an oversized man's long-sleeve shirt. She answers the phone and sits down provocatively.)

(Dick looks over at the woman and begins to sit up, while Richard looks straight ahead and talks into the phone.)

Annie *(In a seductive voice.)* Hello.

Richard Hello, Annie?

Dick *(Heard only by Richard.)* My God, she is hot.

Annie   Richard?

Richard   Yes, it's me. How did you know?

Annie   Because you have a very distinctive and powerful voice.

(Dick excitedly slaps Richard on the back as if to congratulate him.)

Richard   Well, thank you. I take that as a compliment.

Annie   I was just thinking about you. *(Crosses her legs.)*

Dick   *(To himself as he continues to look at Annie.)* I love it. Look at those legs *(Sitting more straight up.)*

Richard   Oh, really, why?

Annie   I just wanted to thank you for last time. I had a really good time. I mean it was really fun. I didn't want to leave. It was good just to talk to a man who seemed to understand a woman and her feelings. I have so much I want to tell you.

Dick   *(To Richard in his ear.)* Tell her you really don't give a shit about anything she has to say and that you really need to see her naked.

Richard   *(To Dick.)* Shush!

Annie   What?

Richard   Oh, sorry, not you. I was swatting away a fly. Yes, it was nice talking to you too. I found your stories of Buffalo

135

really interesting. So much different from how I grew up. I'd love to hear more. So what are you doing?

Annie Now?

Richard Yes

Annie Just chilling out. Getting out of my work clothes and getting ready to take a long shower. It was so hot today. I got all sweaty and sticky. Nothing I put on is comfortable. I'm going to take a cold shower and stand under my fan, totally naked, until I dry off. That would feel so good.

(Annie stands and unbuttons a part of her shirt and rubs her shoulder softly. Dick takes notice and stands up firmly.)

Richard Now, that's where I would like to be a fly on your wall.

Annie Umm. If you were a fly on my wall, mister … you would be in for the time of your life. Flies have it so good sometimes. *(Flirtatiously.)* You only had a little taste last time. The prize is still in the box.

Dick *(Standing up, stretching, flexing his muscles.)* Yes! Yes! Oh my God, this is too good to be true.

Richard *(Amused.)* The prize? Do I get a prize?

Annie You might, but you have to earn it.

Richard Well, how do I know what I'm fighting for?

Annie *(Provocatively.)* Oh, I think you know what you're

fighting for. I see you looking. I know what you want …
what every man wants … and I know how to deliver. You
may have more on your plate than you can handle.

Richard Oh, really!

Annie Really!

*(Dick is jumping up and down and begins to flex his
muscles like a body builder.)*

Richard Be prepared.

Annie I'm always prepared.

Richard No limits?

Annie Hah! I guess we'll have to find out.

*(Dick continues his antics, doing pushups and
singing, "When you're a jet you're a jet all the way
from your first cigarette to you last dying day.")*

Richard *(To Dick.)* Will you stop?

Annie What?

Richard Oh, nothing … just the fly again. You're funny.

Annie *(Laughing and changing moods.)* Thanks, I know I
can fool with you. I like that about you.

Richard *(Looking for words.)* So how are you feeling?

Annie Pretty good except for …

Richard *(Interrupting.)* I was wonder …

Annie Except, I have these really bad cramps, you know, from my period. I feel like I'm about to explode I'm so bloated. It's certainly a lot worse than last month.

Dick *(Immediately sits down in a collapse, utterly disappointed. He begins to slump over on the couch to the point where his head is almost in his lap.)* I knew it. Damn it! Hang up!

Annie Oh, sorry, I'm sure that's more information than you want. What were you about to say?

Richard *(Dick is pestering him with hand jesters.)* Oh, ah, yeah, ah … I lost my train of thought.

Dick Tell her next week.

Richard Oh, I just wanted to say thanks for … ah … last time also. It was fun.

Annie That was it?

Richard *(Trying to stop Dick from pestering him.)* Yes. Thanks. We'll have to do it again sometime.

Annie *(Disappointed and confused.)* Yes. Sometime.

Richard Maybe next week?

Annie Maybe.

Richard Okay … I'll talk to you.

Annie   Well … okay.

Richard   Have a good night.

Annie   Yeah, sure.

Richard   Bye.

(Annie hangs up and leaves. Richard also hangs up.)

Richard   See what you did?

Dick   *(Fully slumped over.)* Did what? It didn't make sense tonight.

Richard   Bull, there were other things we could have done.

Dick   Like what?

Richard   Like you don't know?

Dick   I guess, but you know I don't like restrictions. Women and this monthly thing of theirs. Just my luck. Who else is there?

Richard   Lorrie?

Dick   No tits.

Richard   Betty?

Dick   No ass.

Richard   Ginger!

Dick   Ginger. No. No, not again.

Richard   Get lost. She's a lot of fun, and she's smart, and she loves to dance. She listens to me talk. She even likes the Yankees.

Dick   She's fun, she's smart, likes the Yankees, but her ass is too big and she dresses like a nun. Where does she buy her bras? At a saddle company?

Richard   She's a big-breasted girl.

Dick   I suppose big has its benefits, but I like things firm.

Richard   She's attractive in her own way. You like her. Admit it!

Dick   Sure I like her, that's obvious, but do we have to do it with the same person all the time? BORING! Variety is the spice of life. I need a new venue every now and then. Show what I can do.

Richard   I don't find Ginger boring.

Dick   *(Pleading.)* What's wrong with something new? Plus, she makes you wear a condom. Do you know how I feel when you put that thing on me? A straightjacket. I have a hard time getting started and realizing my full potential. I end up splashing everything all over myself, and no one ever gets to see. My best moments are supposed to be projecting forward. *(Standing up and posing muscularly.)* Showing the world what's inside me … have her screaming for more and more, "Yes! Yes!" And release into the abyss. I have an image to protect, you know.

Richard   Quit complaining.

Dick   I'm not complaining. It's just that …

Richard   *(Ignoring Dick's plea.)* Maybe I'll invite her over and we'll watch the game … get some pizza. Listen to some music afterward. What was that joke she told me? Ah! I remember. She's funny.

Dick   I'm not going to convince you, am I?

Richard   No. But you know I'll take care of you. You're my best friend.

Dick   I know, but take care of me <u>during</u> not after.

Richard   I'll try my best, but we have to be civilized about these things.

Dick   Civilized. Yes … I know … that's too bad. Okay, I'm game.

Richard   *(Grabs his phone and dials her number.)* Hello Ginger, it's Richard. How are you? *(Stands up and paces a bit before starting to take off his shirt. He makes small talk. Richard follows in tandem but half-erect.)*

Dick   *(As they exit and while Richard is on the phone.)* Let me ask you just one favor … it's not a big thing … just a favor, that's all … for me, just this once … I was thinking ….

(They exit.)

End.

Cross Roads

Time: Now.

Setting: Bare stage, dim lighting. A man in his 40s or 50s is standing alone at the front of the stage. Behind him, in the shadows and almost offstage, is another man standing quietly as if presiding over the area. Both are facing the audience. The man in front is unaware of the figure behind.

(Lights come up on the front of the stage.)

Man *(Begins to pace anxiously across the front of the stage.)* Is this it? Is this all there is? Am I who I am and nothing more? It can't be. It just can't be. ... I really don't know exactly what it is that's plaguing me. All I know is that there has got to be something more. There has got to be something else. I'm lost. I'm going around in a dizzying circle. I can't stay here. I know that. I need to get out of here. Get out of here soon—real soon But I don't know how or where to go. I need some help, someone to give me directions.

(The lights go up on the figure in the back.)

Guide   Perhaps I can help.

Man   *(Turning around.)* Where did you come from?

Guide   I've always been here.

Man   You have?

Guide   Yes.

Man *(Moving closer.)* Can you give me directions?

Guide Yes. Where is it exactly that you want to go?

Man That's my point. I don't know. What are the choices?

Guide There are lots of choices. Choose any road you wish.

(He extends his arm scanning over an entire area from the extreme left to the extreme right.)

Man But which one is best?

Guide All these roads travel in different directions. Some are uphill, straight and narrow, while others are more adventurous.

Man Where do they go?

Guide They all arrive at a different place. What is your destination?

Man Anywhere! Just out of here. Out of this blue funk that I can't escape from. Will any of these roads let me do that?

Guide Some will. Some may not. Some will not.

Man Well, I definitely don't want the one that "will not." Where do the other ones go?

Guide You never know exactly.

Man Do they not have a destination?

Guide Not always. Some are not finished. On some you

will have to turn back. Sometimes the trip is all you get.

Man   So tell me. Help me out a bit. *(Pointing straight ahead.)* If I go straight, where will I go? What's out there?

Guide   That's the road you are already on. You can go straight and continue on. I think you know the way. It's the easiest, hardly any twists and turns. Lots of rest stops along the way. Many people follow that road, sometimes without thinking. It's heavily populated by those who don't know nor want to know their destination.

Man   What happens when I get to the end?

Guide   It may be very familiar. You may have been there before. You may be there now. Is this the direction that you want to go?

Man   No, I don't think so. There has to be a better road.

Guide   It's a good, safe road.

Man   Yes, I think I know that. I even think I know the way, but I've been there before, and if I continue, I'll end up exactly in the same place I'm in now.

Guide   You may at that.

Man   No. I don't want that. I'm looking for something more.

Guide   Then that is not the way.

Man   What about the other choices?

Guide   Well, the road to the left is quite interesting.

Man   What will I find out there? Where will I end up? Give me a hint.

Guide   Take a look.

(They step to the side and two young adults, One and Two, enter and walk to the center.)

One   No one has seen nor heard from him for ten years now. He just disappeared.

Two   No hint of where he went. No hint of where he is. No reason why.

One   Didn't talk to anyone. Didn't say word. He seemed okay to me.

Two   No sign of any problems, at least nothing that would lead us to suspect ... suspect that he would find it necessary to leave everything and everybody behind. Mom never got over it.

One   Neither have I.

Two   Nor I.

One   He never saw what I accomplished. What I've done.

Two   Never met his grandchildren.

One   And they never met him.

Two   I wonder if I ever did. Was it all an act? Maybe he never did give a damn. Maybe we were a burden?

One   He destroyed our family.

Two   Made it hard on everyone.

One   Unfair.

Two   Very unfair.

One   Mom died in the agony of not knowing.

Two   All alone with her doubts.

One   I don't like him now.

Two   I hate him.

One   Do you think he's dead?

Two   It doesn't really matter, does it?

(The man bursts out moving again into the center of the stage, with the guide close by. One and Two exit.)

Man   NO! No! No! That's not what I want. I would never do that. Who would ever do that?

Guide   Desperate people do desperate things.

Man   Family has always been my priority. Even if I had to sacrifice. Even if I had to suffer. I am and will always be responsible for what I've created, those who rely on me, who trust me. I would never. Their accomplishments are mine; I share their joy; I feel their heartache. They need me. I need to be there for them. I always have. … Haven't I?

Guide   Have you?

Man   Yes, why do you say otherwise?

Guide   What did they learn from you?

Man   Responsibility! How to live by the rules.

Guide   Whose rules are they?

Man   The rules that normal people live by.

Guide   Normal?

Man   Yes, ordinary people.

Guide   Did you wish your children to be "ordinary"?

Man   No, of course not. You're missing the point.

Guide   I think not. *(Pause.)* See the road to the right. That road may contain wealth and power. More wealth and power than you could have ever dreamed of accomplishing.

Man   Wealth and power! They go hand in hand, don't they? I mean, if you have wealth you automatically have power. If you have wealth, you can buy anything, do anything, go anywhere. Influence … you can buy influence … be famous. What man doesn't want that? Ah! But just how do I get there? That's every person's dream. Just how do I go about doing that? Will that road show me how? Because if it's about money, fame, and fortune, I'm all for it.

Guide   You are?

Man   Yes, of course.

Guide   Take a look.

(They step aside and two prison guards enter.)

Guard One   See the old man in there? Condemned for years now. Just rotting away. He once owned several companies on Wall Street ... employed thousands. At one point, he was worth several millions of dollars. Had everything money could buy.

Guard Two   Well, he sure doesn't have it now. Look at him. All alone. Never any visitors. No one ever calls him. He's just one pathetic-looking convicted felon. What happened?

Guard One   He got greedy. Everything was about money. The more he had, the more he needed. At first, he was legitimate, did some good things, but it never was enough. Never enough. Lie, cheat, and steal. He lied to his family and friends, stole from people who trusted him, and in the end cheated himself.

Guard Two   If he had so much money, couldn't he have bought his way out?

Guard One   Not him. People hated him. He took everything from them. Was the type of guy you hang in effigy. He had no friends, just enemies. His family was embarrassed by him ... disowned him. When he slipped up, everyone pounced on him.

Guard Two   Showed him no mercy.

Guard One   Because he never gave any.

Guard Two   No compassion.

Guard One   It was all about money. Money, money, money. He had so much, it had no value.

Guard Two   Look where it got him. Can't spend it in here. *(Sarcastic laugh.)* He can't even count it.

Guard One   That's a shame. What a waste.

Guard Two   For everyone. He left a legacy of hurt.

(The man bursts out moving again into the center of the stage, with the guide close by. The guards exit.)

Man   No! No! No! That's not what I want. Besides, I don't have that type of skill, to ever get that far.

Guide   You never know about the skills. You may have some that you don't even know you have. You may be surprised every once in a while.

Man   Skills … yeah, I wish. Nothing special about me. *(Beat.)* Does every road have to have a consequence?

Guide   Always. Sometimes the consequences are unintended. Sometimes they are beyond control.

Man   I just thought that having money—lots of money— would let you enjoy things. Do things you never did.

Guide   It can, but it's not the whole answer. Sounds like you won't find what you are looking for if all you want is money.

Man No, I guess you are right about that. Too stressful anyway. I don't want any more stress. Come to think of it, I have more money than I really need anyway. I don't want to worry about how to make more.

Guide Less stress, huh? Well, you know, that there is a road where all you do is relax. Enjoy what you have accomplished. Pass the time away ... play some golf ... go to the beach ... watch baseball games, TV game shows ... eat all the junk food you want. You can sleep all day. Why, some days you don't even have to get up. There's no reason to.

Man A couch potato! No, I don't want to be a couch potato. Wasting away into intellectual nothingness, not being able to have a meaningful conversation. Feeling guilty that everyone around me is being productive while I lie around on the couch second-guessing Joe Torre's pitching rotation and watching Sienfeld reruns. No! Not for me. *(Beat.)* I'll get fat, be bored, and be jealous of everyone around me. People would ask me, "What do you do for a living?" I'd say to them, "Nothing, I don't do a thing." No, that is what I'm trying to escape from. *(Beat.)* You see, I have this creative side to me that I feel I need to explore. I need to make an impact. A positive one. Sure, I want to enjoy whatever time I have left, but I still want to be productive and make an impact. I want to be remembered and be a model for those around me. Leave a legacy that is worthy of being passed on.

Guide But you say you don't like the road you are on.

Man No. No excitement anymore. No challenge. No reward. Everything is the same. Every day is like every other.

Guide Umm. I see. *(Beat.)* Do you know that you don't always have to stay on the pavement?

Man   You mean, sort of like walking in the woods? I'll get lost.

Guide   Not if you keep the main road within sight.

Man   That road. *(Pointing.)* The one that is straight ahead. Does it contain everything and everybody I know and love?

Guide   It does.

Man   Will I remember all that I have accomplished?

Guide   Yes.

Man   I have done some good things.

Guide   You have. Why give it up? Why not build on it?

Man   Why is right. But suppose … just suppose that I walk off the beaten path for a bit. Will I have the chance to do all the things I've always wanted to do? Or try the things I never thought I could?

Guide   That's up to you. What's stopping you?

Man   Good question. *(Thinking.)* Nothing! Nothing is stopping me except my own fear. What if I fail?

Guide   So what if you do?

Man   The main road is always within view, is it not?

Guide   Yes, you can always find your way back.

Man   Umm, so it doesn't really matter if I fail. In fact, I can try again. Do it again. *(Beat.)* And if I succeed, well …that's it, isn't it? That's it. I just have to give myself the chance, be all I can be without sacrificing all that I am. Whatever I learn, I can bring back to others. Encourage them to walk off the path. How far is up to them. Convince them that life is not confined to a path or a script. Convince them that life is about experience and enjoyment and love. To love and be loved, to share the moments, to encourage those near to you to do the same. Yet always remember the way back and that someone will always be there.

> *(He starts to walk straight ahead but turns before he exits.)*

Man   Time to put my boots on and clear a path in the woods. Thanks. You know, I can't seem to recall your name. My memory slips sometimes.

Guide   My name? My name is easy to remember. It's the same as yours.

> *(The man exits.)*

> *(The guide steps forward and speaks to the audience.)*

Guide   What about you? What about each and every one of you? Are you now thinking of all the things you want to do but have convinced yourself you can't? What would happen if you erase the "can't" from the proposition and substitute, "I can"? Or at least, "I'll try"?

End.

Characters and Casting

Character	Description	Originating Actor

The Fourth Voice

Debbie	Single, professional, smart, late 20's-30's	Meghan Kulig
Voice One	Voice of security and companionship, female 20's	AC Jermyn
Voice Two	Voice of motherhood, late 40's-50's	Barbara Miluski
Voice Three	Voice of promiscuity, female 20's-30's	Emily Zech

Changing Times

Jay	Married, optimistic, romantic, age denial, 50's	Paul Trupia
Jane	Married, self conscience, pessimistic,50's	Carole Boniece
Couple	Young lovers, non speaking	Judith Kilzer, Lee Cavellier

A Day at the Office

Bob	Old line manager, insecure, unaware, 50's	John Naughton
Sophie	Secretary, sarcastic, not helpful, 30's	Vesna Ivkovic
Mike	Aggressive young professional 20's-30's	Lee Cavellier
Janet	Pandering, knows how to use her sex, 20's- 30's	Jessica Barrington
John	The big boss. Wide age range	Henri Douvry

Going to Paris

Man	Single, professional, lonely, late 40's-50's	Paul Trupia
Conductor	Male, stereotypical train conductor, 50+	Kevin O'Brien
Woman	Single, romantic, encouraging, late 40's-50's	Sheilah Spagnoli

The Last Word

Rosa	Devoted and caring wife and mother, late 40's-50's	Mel Squires
Maria	Single, energetic, fashionable, independent, 20's	Mona Persson
Alfredo	Old fashioned, stubborn, demanding, late 40's-50's	James Heaphy

Daydreams

Henry	Married, timid, unfulfilled, dreamer, 50's	Anthony Allutto
Catherine	Married, dominating, demanding, 50's	Barbara Miluski
Young Man	Young and attractive 30's	Frankie Gonzolez

A Matter of Choice

Lynn	Single, provocative, a bit insecure, late 30's	Carol Boniece
Frank	Single, unaware, man about town, 40's-50's	Kevin O'Brien
Anna	Single, religious, intolerant, plain, late 40's-50's	Eileen Landers

The Hired Hand

Linda	Divorced, self reliant, demanding, to the point, 40's	Sheilah Spagnoli
Julie	Single, good friend, concerned, realistic, 30's	Maureen Chandler
Peter	Single, well spoken, confident, 30's- 40's	Matt Fitzgerald

Diplomacy

Linda	The President of the USA, demanding, caring, concerned, wife and mother, late 40's-50's	Sheilah Spagnoli
Carl	The General, formal, aggressive, bitter, 50's	Paul Trupia
Don	The Secretary of State, practical, naïve, concerned, 50's	Richard Cozart

The Best of Friends

Richard	Average, single hard working male 30's-40's	Hunter Tremayne
Dick	Penile personification 30's-40's	Mick Fickey
Annie	Attractive, flirtatious, late 20's-30's	Judith Kilzer

Cross Roads

Man	Married, responsible family man, confused, unrewarded, 40's-50's	Jim Heaphy
Guide	Voice of alternatives, can be male or female various ages	Matt Gologor
Others	Wide variety	Marisa Trupia, Rob Aloi, Kevin O'Brien,

Targeted Audience

• Actors

• Acting Schools and Classes

• Universities

• Small Theatre Companies, Local Theatre Groups

• Play Festivals.

• Other Playwrights and Directors

• Those in the 40-50 year old range who will find the content something that they can relate to.

To the actor, acting coach, producer or director, the collection offers an array of characters, ages, situations, genre and range to allow the development and showcase of talent. The real life situations are familiar to many and allow the performers to identify with and interpret the role as they may see it. The collection features realistic dialogue and monologues that have been used as material for auditions. The scripts, combined with acting talent, effective direction and technical support have in resulted in a productions that are creative, entertaining and thought provoking.